THE
SOUL OF CAMBRIA

in the days of Caradoc
King of Siluria
A.D. XXXVI

By
E. J. MACAULAY

A REPRINT OF 1931 EDITION BY
COVENANT PUBLISHING COMPANY, BRITAIN

PUBLISHED BY
ARTISAN SALES
P.O. BOX 1497 • THOUSAND OAKS
CALIF. 91360 U.S.A.

COPYRIGHT ©1989 BY ARTISAN SALES
ALL RIGHTS RESERVED

ISBN: 0-934666-28-8
LIBRARY OF CONGRESS CATALOG CARD NUMBER: 88-71795

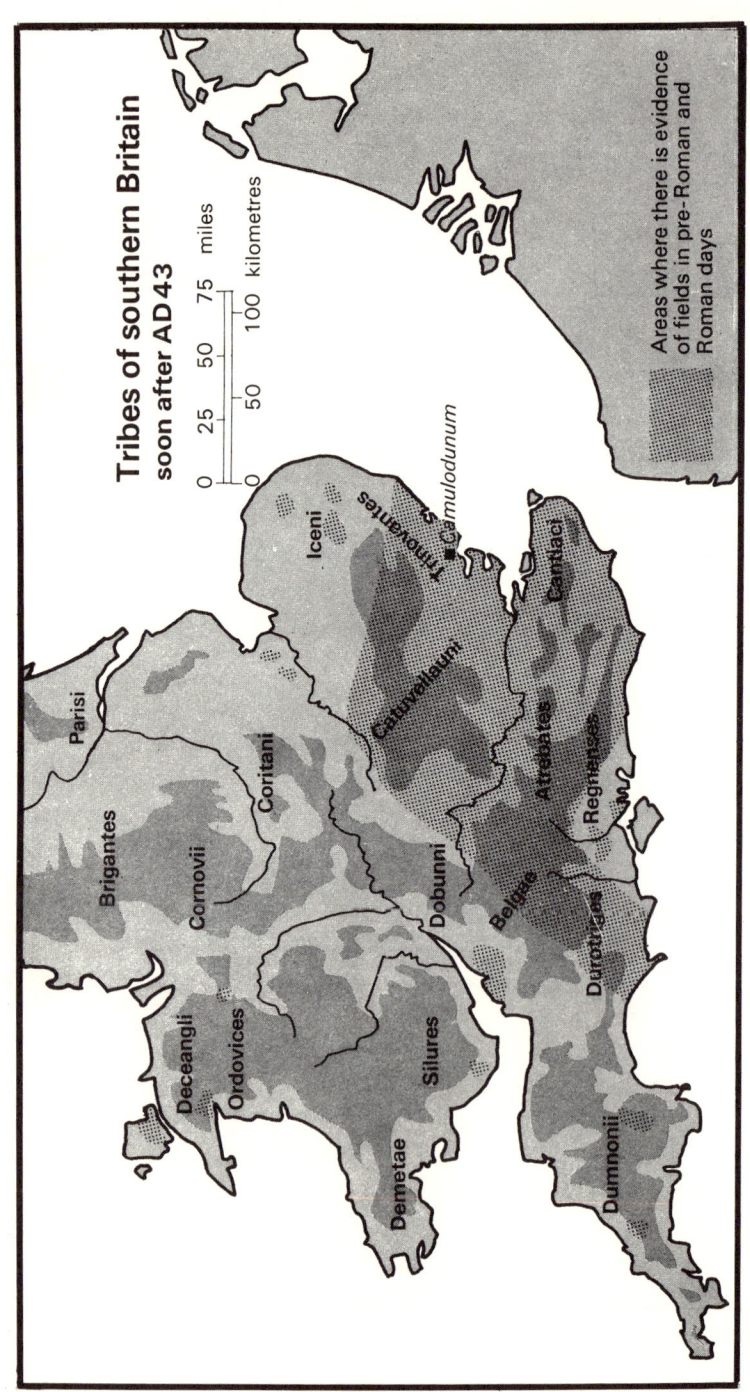

CONTENTS

Who is Who 5

Preface 7

PART I

Chap.
- I DAWN 9
- II TYRE 11
- III GWALD YR HÂV 17
- IV CHRISTIANITY VERSUS DRUIDISM 21
- V KING CARADOC OF SILURIA 31
- VI "THE DOMUS DEI" 39
- VII QUEEN AREGWEDD — CARTISMANDUA . 47
- VIII SENATOR AULUS RUFUS PUDENS PUDENTIUS . 54
- IX USK CASTLE 60
- X PRINCESS EURGAIN 63
- XI KIN CARADOC'S BETRAYAL 69
- XII PRINCESS GLADYS 73

PART II

- I PALATIUM BRITANNICUM 83
- II CASTELLO SAMNIUM 91
- III BISHOP LINUS (PRINCE LLEYN) A.D. 90 . 99

PART III

NOTES 109
BIBLIOGRAPHY 128

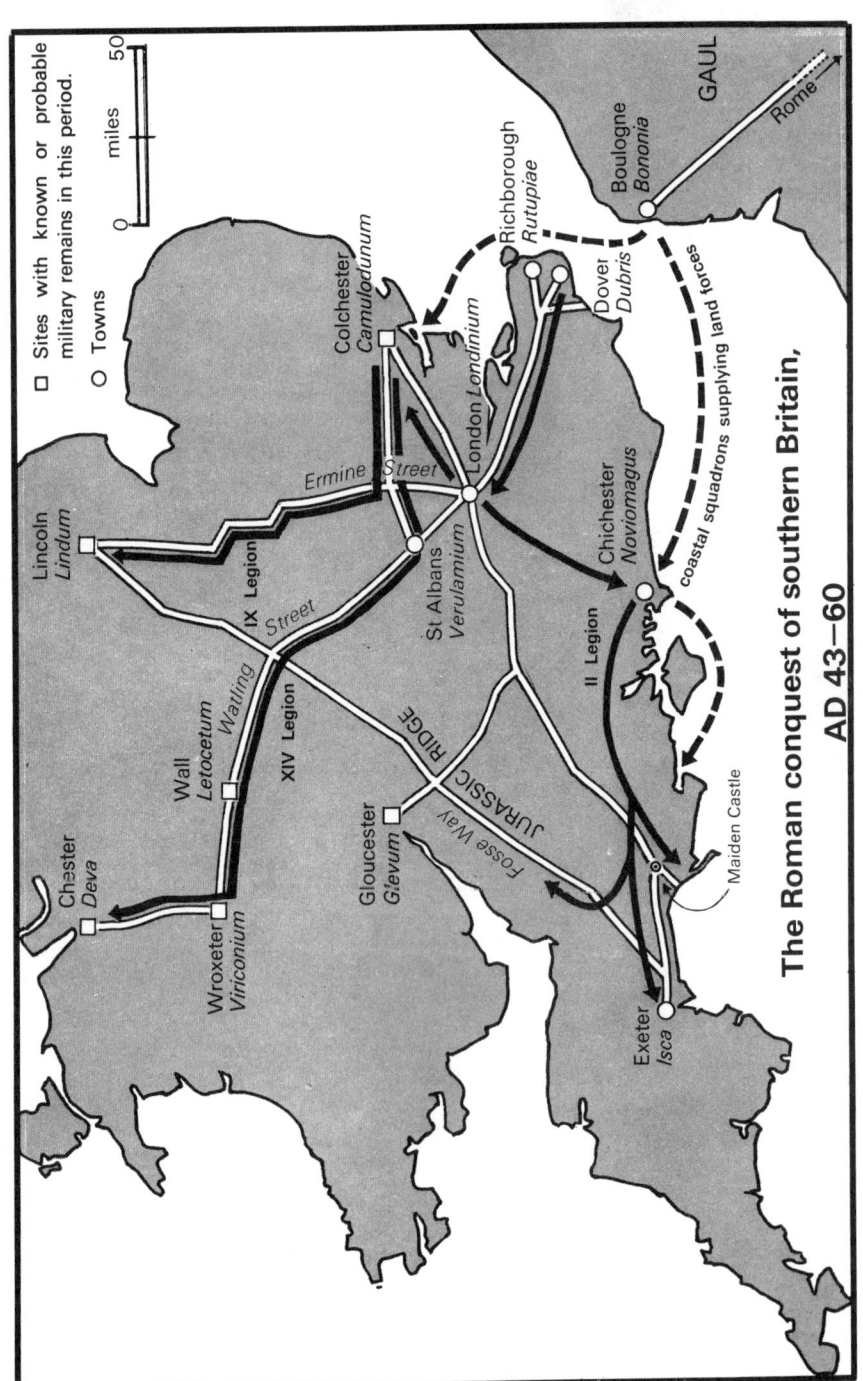

WHO IS WHO?

THE WELSH ROYAL FAMILY

Bran or Brennus, King of Siluria, resigned the Silurian crown to Caradoc and became Arch-Druid of Caerleon-upon-Usk.

King Caradoc (Caractacus) son of the Arch-Druid Bran, was elected Pendragon.

CHILDREN OF KING CARADOC

Sons	Daughters
Prince Cyllin or Cyllinus	Princess Eurgain
Prince Lleyn or Linus	Princess Gladys-Claudia
Prince Cynon	

Prince Lylen—Linus, second son, became first Bishop of Rome.

Princess Eurgain, eldest daughter—first female saint of Britain, married Lord Salog (Salisbury), a Roman Patrician.

Princess Gladys, second daughter, renamed Claudia, married Senator Aulus Rufus Pudens Pudentius; owner of a residence at Chichester, and large possessions in Samnium Umbria (Italy). they were married in A.D. 53, in Rome. They probably met at Regnum, the old name for Chichester.

There is a tablet in Chichester Museum which was probably in a temple dedicated to "Neptune et Minervae." The temple appears to have been erected about A.D. 50, before, of course, the conversion of Pudens or his marriage to Claudia.

CHILDREN OF SENATOR PUDENS AND PRINCESS CLAUDIA

Sons	Daughters
St. Timotheus	St. Pudentiana
St. Novatus	St. Praxedes

MARTYRS

King Arviragus, "cousin of King Caradoc," a Druid.

King Arviragus was brother to Guiderius, who was killed at

Wimbledon Heath, and succeeded him. Such an emergency required the establishment of the pendragonate, or military dictatorship. Caradoc was unanimously elected to that high office, Arviragus was first to give his vote in favor of Caradoc and consent to serve under him.

"Hath our great enemy Arviragus, the Car bourne British king, dropped from his battle throne?"

Morgan.

PREFACE

"Everything unknown is doubted."

A Welsh Adage.

"The Soul of Cambria" is a purely imaginary romance of scattered fragments of history and legend, threaded together as shells on the shore of time. For the names of these heroes and heroines have survived the centuries.

Whatever merit there is, is due almost entirely to The Reverend R. W. Morgan's "St. Paul in Britain" and the exhaustive research of others.

Whatever may or may not have been in the lives of those who centuries ago passed "within the veil," they won — in some cases after martyrdom — Eternal Life.

One and all seem to have stood staunchly in the faith they had accepted, and in Him they believed and loved unto death. They swerved not from the fiery trial when life itself had to be surrendered in order to uphold their ideals.

As peaks in a mountain range appear between drifting clouds, so we catch fleeting glimpses of these heroic men and women through historical and legendary mists. God rest their souls.

> "When our Land see truth in Legends
> That sustained her in the past,
> And our people view their Sires
> As no longer fools and liars;
> > Then behold
> > Dross turned to gold,
> Branches, Root and Royal Stem
> Meet for Him of Bethlehem."

NOTE: The original edition (1931) has conversations in archaic Old English. In this revised edition (1989), conversations are in modern English.

CHAPTER I

DAWN

DAWN was breaking into day over the Galilean hills which stand around Nazareth, rousing slumbering workers.

In an archway lit with the gold of morning stood a graceful woman. By her blue embroidered robe we know she was not a native of Nazareth, but of "the city of David." She wore her silver marriage coins and they reflected the golden rays. She stood in statuesque stillness, lost in thought, gazing over the distant hills, her left hand toying with the tendrils of a magnificent vine which clung to the walls. There was more than beauty in her placid face; there was strength of character and sweetness of dispositon, depicting a perfectly balanced woman, a very gracious personality. Suddenly her eyes filled and she clasped her hands to her breast, and looking up, she murmured, "Your Will be done. Yes, Lord, Hannah was a grave woman. You, God did give her little Samuel in answer to her prayers. She, too, must have suffered and shed tears at parting when she left him at Shiloh. Shall I be less brave? No, God help me." Hastily she brushed aside her tears and lifting her water jar on to her shoulder, started toward the well when she heard her name.

"Mary, where are you going, beloved child?" Advancing toward her over the stony path, his long graceful robes sweeping the oleander blossoms, walked a man. She placed her water jar on the ground, and moved slowly toward him.

"You are early, Uncle Joseph, and the day is young."

"Fair daughter, you know well what brings me here."

She hung her head, and as she tried to reply, tears trembled on her long lashes. He laid his hand on her shoulder.

"I know what it will mean to you, beloved one, dear little mother, but be brave."

"Uncle, He is such a Son, and it is so hard to part. Must we?"

"Dear child, He knows best and will decide."

"Yes, but it seems so far and the days will be so long and lonely with dangers, too, by ..."A slim Boy quietly joined them, and seeing His Mother's sorrowful face, took her hand in His.

He was perfect in features and form, lovely in all that makes perfection. His rich auburn hair fell away from His noble forehead in waves. His eyes rested in quiet impelling power on the troubled ones of His suffering mother.

Mary laid her arm around His shoulder and gazed at the Son whom God had entrusted to her care, and she grew calm as they waited for Him to speak.

"Didn't you know that I must be about My Father's business?"

THE GLASTONBURY HYMN

"And did those feet in ancient time
Walk upon England's mountains green?
And was the Holy Lamb of God
On England's pleasant pastures seen?
And did the countenance Divine
Shine forth upon our clouded hills?
And was Jerusalem builded here
Among those dark satanic mills?

"Bring me my sword of burning gold!
Bring me my arrows of desire!
Bring me my spear! O clouds unfold!
Bring me my chariot of fire!
I will not cease from mental fight,
Nor shall my sword sleep in my hand,
Till we have built Jerusalem
In England's green and pleasant land."

by William Blake

CHAPTER II

TYRE

What was left of the once renowned city of Tyre lay peacefully in the arms of the still blue water, beneath the rays of a fierce sun.

Soon after the tragic death of Israel's King, a small caravan might have been seen approaching the Causeway, which had been constructed for Alexander the Great in order to conquer the brave natives. Alexander stopped at nothing, for the lust of power held him in its avaricious grip. What were the elegant decorated pillars of the temples of Hercules and Io, where the Phoenician nobility and kings in ages past paraded the colonnaded courtyards or loggias, robed in magnificent silken robes? For Tyre was no mean rival to the court of the Pharaohs, only perhaps losing some of its reputation. In ages before, Egypt, at the zenith of her power, could boast of advanced enlightenment and intellectual development. So it was in the days when Moses was cradled in the reed ark, saved to fulfil his destiny as an Israelite leader, with knowledge of ancient lore that only such men as the priests of old could impart.

Vanished as a dream were the royal galleys that left the harbor, propelled by chained slaves. These Argosies were gorgeous with gilt and many colors which were reflected in the blue water. Melting colors tinted the wavelets that the great boat made as it cut its way along bringing tin and lead from the Britannia Mendips.

On the shore fishing nets were spread out drying. The Fisher-folk were gossiping, seated on fragments of pillars, watching events with interest. For already it was known who the Man was who was about to embark in the large vessel anchored far out, resting on the waters of the dangerous harbor which concealed some of the hidden glories beneath the seaweeds.

"Tyre, once the queen of the commercial world," built on a small island; (David Roberts —"The Holy Land.") is protected on the west by high cliffs that resist the fury of the angry sea. It is a singularly small territory to maintain the mightiest traffic of the ancient world, which extended through Persia, through India and westward through the ocean. Northward it reached the British Isles — the tin and wolfskins of Britain met the gold and silk of the remote East in the marts of Tyre.

It was here Hiram the king of Tyre dwelt, who sent cedar-trees from Lebanon to King Solomon for the Temple in Jerusalem. "The fleet of Hiram was to Solomon an important source of wealth." And what picturesque scenes would glow with color as "twenty measures of pure oil" and "wheat for food" were sent in return from the City of David.

Again, think of this little city during Shalmaneser's invasion 720 B.C., or of avaricious Nebuchadnezzar, whom the brave natives resisted for thirteen years.

Did the feet of the Son of Man enter this city? We are not told. Had He done so, He would have seen the doom the prophet predicted fulfilled to the letter.

A native crowd gathered around the weary camels. Some of the men gaped open-mouthed as they minutely examined the bales into which they thrust grimy fingers. They were clad in humble robes, and not as their forefathers, in "Purple and blue." The mariners, descendants of "Zidon and Arvad," were hoisting a great sail to the mast "taken from (the) cedars (of) Lebanon." The days were no more when "the fine linen with embroidered work from Egypt was that which thou spreadest forth to be thy sail."

The great water jars had been freshly filled at the fountain, and were being hoisted up, together with the crates of citrons and dates.

"It is Joseph the Merchant who sails," said a venerable Hebrew, willing to air his knowledge to a late arrival, as he stroked his long beard.

"He's the one who used to sit on our High Council of the Sanhedrin. An Honorable Counselor indeed!" Then, becoming very mysterious, he whispered loudly in his deaf friend's ear: "Yes! and he went to Pilate to ask for the dead body of a man they call our King, defiling himself according to our law, and he is still defiled! Had that imposter whom they call 'The King of the Jews' lived, do you think our nation would have accepted him? No, He was no king. He never sat on the throne of David or Solomon, nor did he ever use the palace. Where is his army? Ill luck has befallen Judah since the fools of our nation forsook the faith of our forefathers to follow him. Bah! Come, let us move off lest we, too, become defiled for I see that merchant traitor and his friends advancing towards us. Curse them all!"

He spat out his feelings and slunk away to watch unseen behind a boat.

The leader was a tall man with fine regular features, singularly striking in appearance. His deepset eyes noted every detail as that of a competent traveller, accustomed to the sea. His high forehead was partially hidden by his Eastern headdress. He leaned on the Thorn staff, which was to become so famous — later in Britain. In the East these staves are considered heirlooms. Now and then he spoke, giving directions until everything was safely on board — great care being taken of the large bales containing Tyrian dyed silks destined for King Arviragus in the "Island of the Mighty."

The preparations were completed when a small cavalcade arrived, four being women. They dismounted and their luggage was piled up by their attendents.

"See, Martha," said a sweet-toned voice, "there is Brother Joseph and there is our ship. I shall call it the Little Ark."

The elder woman smiled and turned to watch the toilers of the deep.

One of the women, clutching a faded bunch of cycalmen, remained gazing back. Deep emotion overwhelmed her lovely face, and she held out a yearning arm towards the land.

Mary of Bethany, realizing her sorrow, quietly slipped her hand under her arm, saying: "Dear, He whom we love is not there now; He is risen."

"Yes, little one, but his land is the soil He trod! It was here, when my heart was broken, that I kissed His feet. It was here He set me free, and cast out the demons which were such a terror. Look, little sister, I think those distant hills are Judea, and behind,

Jerusalem, where we watched Him die!" A shudder shook her. "There, too, in the Garden where I first saw Him alive — and then His farewell on the Mount of Olives."

"My dear, this land will become a memory to us, but to others who remain, it will become a terror, as He predicted."

Silent tears rolled down, leaving a shining line on her cheeks.

"And none of us can ever return. Rome has planted its power in our land, and Caesar will not rest until the city is subdued and desecrated. We are hunted by the soldiers, hated by our own people, and in danger everywhere."

Thus they stood, searching the misty distance, before they turned west to face sacrifice and obey His command to tell others of their Friend — their King.

They sailed into the golden pathway of a setting sun. The land of Israel was wrapped in a purple haze, above which gleamed the snowy uplands of Lebanon.

So they came to Marseilles. ("The Coming of the Saints," Taylor.)

After some time spent in France, it was necessary that this little company should separate. St. Joseph of Arimathea, with the intention of Christianizing our ancestors, decided to trek north.

"In Christ's own harvest field, we bid farewell for ever
And yet, with all its sadness, strangely sweet
Was this our parting: for the Comforter
Had crept into our hearts and gladdened them
With subtle whispers of the Infinite
As Spirit speaks to spirit — seems to say
'There is no parting unto them that have
Their habitation in Eternity:
The Spirit is not subject unto Time,
And naught can from this knowledge sever those
Whose names are written in the Book of Life.'
And so they made their passage perilous
Of that wide strait that doth divide the lands,
Four laboured on the tossing seas,

> Taking the oars within a merchant's boat
> Until at last they made the Cornish coast,
> Where the great rock of Ictis jutteth out
> Encircled by the waters; and from thence
> Westward, then north, along a barren shore
> In poverty and hunger made their needs
> Was by a band of miners offered them
> In barter for the labour of their hands.
> So for a season, tinmen they became;
> No legend is, but warranted by truth!
>
> Glastonbury Script.

So, wearied with the journey and burdened with their tents and what had been saved, they came at last within sight of Inis Vytren. (An ancient Celtic name for Glastonbury.)

Away over marsh wastes the Tor rose up in solitary majesty, undoubted monarch over all smaller hills.

Nestling at its foot were the wattle huts of the natives. It was here St. Joseph intended to dwell, and build —

> "A shrine which never shall of gold be built,
> Nor yet of silver metal, but of Faith;
> So shall it not be subject to decay,
> But being built of Faith, shall aye endure."
>
> Glastonbury Script.

However, between them and the coveted resting place lay the shallow Meare waters.

But the villagers had seen them, and a long oak canoe grooved out of a solid tree was laboriously paddled through the deeper channels towards the pilgrims.

The rowers paused, suspiciously scanning the strangers. Having satisfied themselves that they came in peace, and after some explanation of a limited kind, they landed them at the little cove where interested groups cautiously approached.

Women's bone needles were held suspended from sewing the skins. Others hurried from their wattle homes, dragging the toddlers along. Some trailed wattle twigs that they were weaving into the baskets which were so prized in Rome, or spun fleecy wool on their wheels. Potters and glassmakers joined their neighbors, suspiciously eyeing the foreigners, and commenting between themselves as to their raiment, which differed considerably from that of Roman custom.

At last all that was saved lay piled around them. They looked round at the solemn hardy Northerners in their rough homespuns and leather girdles, bare feet, and wild hair; smelling of peat smoke. The fitful winter sun shone forth to give them a shy greeting It was obscured behind gray misty clouds, which scudded before a cold north-west wind and moved over the Mendips like feathers — a cold chilly reception, so unlike their sun-baked native land. It would have taken more than this to make them relinquish their objective. They asked for the chief and learned with difficulty that he was a long way off. But they were pointed to a spot where they might pitch their tents. Then they knelt on the short grass. The wind played round them; their long beards were softly blown about their throats. The Leader uttered strange words, the natives thought. But God heard, and God blessed that little group of earnest pilgrims, the first Christian pioneers who ever landed on our shore.

There seemed little chance of much happening while the wintry blasts swept over the cold Meare meadows, the wind whistling through the rushes. They were shown a spot and allowed to erect their tents.

St. Joseph of Arimathea and a few intimate ones climbed up the lower hill, and on Wyrall, the Saint thrust into the soft earth his precious staff. (which blossoms at Christmastide, mindful of Our Lord)

Tradition is, we hope, founded on fact. Whether this is so or not, the Holy thorn has been preserved and cultivated through centuries by Glastonbury lovers, and it decorates the altars in St. John's parish church, at the Christmas festival.

CHAPTER III

GWLAD YR HÂV[1]

A fierce sun poured down on Camelot, famous because of its association with King Arthur and his Knights. The still air was alive with winged insects. Farm dogs stretched out limply in the shade, snapping at flies.

The inn-keeper's wife slumbered on the ivy-covered porch, dreaming of a Prince Charming, and probably, a very significant palace.

A clatter of hoofs suddenly roused them all. Dame Martin, blinking stupidly, was dismayed to behold a large cavalcade men-at-arms. Her hired hands were away because haymaking was in full swing.

A handsome fellow in the heyday of his manhood, and evidently the leader, flung off his jaunty cap, little mindful of the feathers he ruffled. Pushing back his flowing locks, he cried: "Aha! Who serves here? Get up, Dame Martin, and beware lest the credit of this hostelry suffer from slackness of service! Bring mead! And bring it quickly or we will surely enter and search for ourselves, and perhaps discover its secret hiding-place. Our throats are choked with dust and as dry as the deserts of Arabia. Were it not for the shade of this noble oak, I'd die quickly. Then there would be trouble indeed, followed by a sad ceremony at a big pit, watered by your tears."

"Young cock-fighter. He speaks like a river in a flood. Who is he to speak to me this way?" she muttered. She speedily filled with liberal hand the horn tankards, which she put down noisily before the men, secretly eyeing the man who had ordered her about with such a voice of authority. Her good man would never have done so, knowing the weight of her fists.

With a certain air of selection, she handed a brimming horn to the young cavalier.

With a twinkle in his eyes, and winking the eye farthest from her, he considerably upset the solemnness of his men.

---
[1] This is intended to allude to Somersetshire, of which "Gwind Yr Hâv" is the Welsh appellation, and with which the etymology of the Havren (Severn) is probably connected. — Mabinogin Notes, p. 334.

"To your health, good woman," he said as he flourished the sparkling liquor aloft and drank to the dregs. He smacked his lip saying, "You will be famous, if you're not already celebrated. It's the best I have ever tasted."

She looked from one tankard to another with dismay, noting her precious hoarded supply quickly diminishing. Her hands on her hips, she looked at the group of hot, good-natured men-at-arms as they sat at ease enjoying the shade, and turning to the young gallant, she said, "You are very bold, young man, and your father has neglected your manners; but your mother, whoever she is, cannot be blamed for your handsome face and if you will pardon my remarks, you have the air of a prince."

A burst of uncontrolled laughter gurgled from the throats of a dozen or more men who with mead cups, tried, but with dire results, to smother their mirth.

Dame Martin was furious, and in suppressed emotion, shook her fists in their faces. Undaunted, she turned towards the young upstart, scowling at him.

"Not that any nobility would come this way — I only wish they would while you are here. Then perhaps you would learn to be civil."

The leader rose. Bowing low in mock ceremony, he replied, "Dame Martin, I am Arviragus, your King." He lightly touched her hand with his lips. She was speechless with horror.

"If I had time to stay here, I would without doubt ask you to become my instructress. We must be up and away; so let us part in peace and friendliness. I mean no offense. We kings need friends, and our subjects need our protection – also better understanding between kings and commoners. The shadows deepen, cast by the winged emblems of a powerful enemy. Farewell. Perhaps we may meet again."

Springing lightly into his saddle, he beckoned to his purse-bearer, whispering, "Deal generously with our hostess."

Soon they were enveloped in a cloud of dust. Dame Martin gazed down the valley. It was a dream come true, for a real Prince Charming had come and gone. It was the most wonderful day of her life.

WYR ISRAEL

The following morning King Arviragus rode into the village of "Ynis Wytrin". The clatter of horses brought the natives out of their wattle dwellings.

The king's quick eye rested inquiringly on the foreigners, and reining in his powerful horse, he beckoned them to approach. St. Joseph of Arimathea was anxious to speak with the king, if he would grant him the favor, and bowed low in his slow Eastern fashion.

The King returned the greeting but something in the stately bearing of the dark-eyed man caused him to dismount, and he approached on foot.

"I am King Arviragus. Where are you from, and why did you come here?"

"Greetings, O King. I am called Joseph the Merchant, from the land of Israel, and my companions are also from there. We have waited some months for permission to become your subjects and to build us warmer shelter than our tents afford. We ask you, O King, to graciously grant us a little land. We are men of peace. We will observe the laws of your kingdom for we are fugitives. Let us, we beg you, find sanctuary, and we will do our best to reward you. The land of God is overrun by Caesar's armies, and you know that they are cruel and unholy men. I am especially hated in Palestine because I believe Jesus Christ is the Messiah. The members of the Sanhedrin do not favor the claims of the Prophet.

"Oh King Arviragus, I wish I could tell you of the wonderful things we witnessed, and how He rose out of the tomb in the early dawn, and appeared to us! Oh, and finally He ascended to the sky, Our King — and rose higher and higher, until we lost sight of Him whom we adored."

He looked up, lost in thought, his eyes lit up. He forgot the king, who would always remember that moment of revelation.

The King bade him farewell and said: "I would hear more, but not now. But how do you think the Druid Brotherhood will act toward you? They are the real rulers. They are religious instructors, and have many Cors. Arch Druid Bran is my uncle, and is here on a visit, and see – he now approaches. I am willing to bestow twelve hides$_1$ of land unto you untaxed; but if I do Bran may object. But I will speak with him, and perhaps he will favor your petition."

While the king and his uncle held council with others of the order, Joseph spread out the rich purple Tyrian silks and ivory caskets destined for this monarch should fate allow them to meet.

The king advanced and said he could find no cause to turn them out of the country and trusted they would in every way consider the rules and abide faithful to the British cause.

Then the merchant pointed to the gifts. The king was entranced by the gorgeous purple color. He asked many questions, and particularly if they were for barter, and from what country.

Joseph smiled and bowing low said, "Nay, O King, they are not for barter or exchange, but hearing good reports of you I desired to bring you these, and offer them to you. Will you accept these trifles?"

"Accept, Joseph the Merchant! What would you think me to be if I refused so magnificent a gift? Verily I'll be the envy of all when I don this splendor in court.

"Joseph converted this King Arviragus
By his prechying to know ye lawes divine
And baptized him as write hath Nennius
The chronicler in Brytain tongue full fyne
And to Christes lawes made hym enclyne
And gave hym then a shield of silver white
A crosse end long, and overthwart full perfite
These armes were used throughout all Brytain
For common syne, each man to know his nacion
And thus his armes by Joseph creacion
Full long afore St. George was generate
Were worshipt here of mykell elder date."

Extracted from "Prehistoric London,"

---

[1] A hide of land is a Saxon measurement. It is the amount deemed adequate for a free family and its dependents; what one could till with one plough in a year. This would be about 120 acres of arable land.

CHAPTER IV

CHRISTIANITY VERSUS DRUIDISM
Triads

"There are three ways of searching the heart of man: in the thing he is not aware of, in the manner he is not aware of, and at the time he is not aware of."

"Grant, O God, Thy refuge;
And in refuge, reason;
And in reason, light;
And in light, truth;
And in truth, justice;
And in justice, love;
And in love, the love of God;
And in the love of God, all
    blessedness and all Goodness."

"Since hallowed pile by simple builders rear'd,
Mysterious round, through distant times rever'd.
Ordained with earth's revolving orb at last,
Thou bringest to light the present and the past.

A few days after King Arviragus and his noisy cavalcade had swept through "Ynis Vytren,"(literally "Glass Island," today Glastonbury) the natives were bidding farewell to their honored ex-Welsh King Bran, Arch Druid of Caerleon-upon-Usk, who had officiated at an assembly as one of the three Arch Druids of Britain at that time.

Among the villagers stood St. Joseph of Arimathea, awaiting his turn to bid him farewell. On meeting they advanced toward a fallen tree and seated themselves in a warm sun-bathed spot.

That the Druid had remarkable intellectual qualifications we know from his subsequent history.

Joseph of Arimathaea, styled in the New Testament "a counsellor," meaning a member of the Jewish Sanhedrin, or supreme Council of the Seventy, was – so tradition records – a merchant, known in Cornwall as "Joseph was in the tin trade." The difference between these men was religious not racial.

The Kelt was probably suspicious of, if not antagonistic to these foreigners, however much conscience protested against a too hasty judgment. There must have been a fear of loss or that something these strangers hinted at, or what they represented, would undermine the ancient stronghold of the Gorsedd ceremonial.

As for the first pioneer, St. Joseph of Arimathea, and his eleven companions, theirs was keen desire to win these prophetic isles over to Christianity.

We hardly value our privilege until we learn that St. Simon Zelotes, then St. Aristobulus, came here. The latter became Britain's first bishop, and a yet greater star of the faith, if this could be said of any in those days, St. Paul himself, as every evidence shows.

A conversation much on the following lines was inevitable, for years later the Druids became prelates of the Christian Church.

The Druid opened fire; he had really nothing to lose, and the Saint had so much to offer him.

Visualise these two in their picturesque robes, seated in the very center of "The Royal Isle" of Druidism — the whole atmosphere Druidic.

Then the able Briton spoke: "You may hope to convert and turn us away from our belief. You might as well attempt to turn the tides from rolling up on our shores!"

"That, O Druid, applies more to our faith. As the ocean waters wash the sands of all continents, so our faith will spread!"

"I note honest and hopeful conviction in thy face, or verily I should deem you the biggest boaster in these isles. We claim a divine source for all we hold sacred.

"Druidism is lost in antiquity. In 'Yinis Witrin,' or if you prefer it — 'The Honey Isle of Beli' — it has flourished for centuries, brought here by one named 'Hu Gadarn,' a contemporary of the great Patriarch Abraham of Ur."

"Our Monoliths stand today in Elam."(Ancient name for Persia.)

"Druids officiate in forty or more Cors in 'The Island of the Mighty'. (Ancient name for Britain) Our universities are renowned for the wisdom and purity of our doctrine. Our fame, as thistledown, has flown across continents, and students from other nations journey here for instruction. Large gatherings assemble at Amberesbi, testifying to the continuity and popularity of our belief."

Joseph regarded him with growing interest, inspired by the knowledge that the Druids were a challenge to evangelize. "Druid brother, I would like to question you about some things. I learned that your official robes are white and very ornate, and they seem wonderfully made, like the Mosaic ones; that they are 'fastened by a belt, and that a Druid's cross is made of gold down the length of the back'. Moreover, your crown is gold-engraved, and harps and trumpets are used; both are familiar to us."

The Arch Druid was surprised.

"That's true, Israelite. Listen — no one but a Druid can offer sacrifices, nor is any candidate admissible to the order who cannot prove his geneology from free parents for nine generations. The order of the blaenorion, or aristocracy, makes us literally a royal priesthood — kings, princes and nobles.

"My family records go back fifteen generations. Consider our national laws and how just they are. We are administrators in addition to being statesmen and bards. Listen to our triads: 'There are three things the safety of which depends on others: the sovereignty, national courage, just administration of the law.'

"There are three duties of every man: worship God, be just to all men, and die for your country."

"Excellent, O Druid, but I would like to ask about sacrificial ceremonies. Have you ever sought some alternative, a substitute or higher ideal?"

"No, why should we? What constituted the center of our belief, which generations of my ancestors practiced, is good enough for us. The valleys are clothed with fresh grass, and let me warn you, stranger, consider our cattle sacred. And what about your sacrifices?"

"True, Druid, we have practiced blood-shedding for centuries, according to Divine instruction to our forefathers, and Moses, our lawgiver. Mankind needed a 'blood covenant'; 'without shedding of blood, there is no remission of sins.' Moreover, it brought men into touch with unseen realities; even more than that — with God Himself. His ordinances were destined to continue until the Perfect One who proceeded from the Almighty Father came, to become the Redeemer of the world. He existed in the bosom of the Deity, one God 'before the world was.' In our day God took our nature, and became incarnate. His coming was foretold by our prophets.

"I say He is 'The Truth,' against the world. Every argument and human reasoning against Him, or His claim, will, as waves beating against a rock, fall back as broken spray. I venture to repeat His words — much like a Triad:

"'I am the way, the truth and the life,' and 'You shall know the truth, and the truth shall make you free.'

"His assertion, 'I am', strikes awe in our hearts, for thus has our 'Ancient of Days' always drawn attention to Himself. And when such an affirmation fell from the lips of his Son — God — man, living in our midst, sharing our daily life, proclaiming His Own Deity, we were amazed; later we believed.

"So for us 'The truth is a Being — God.'"

The Druid's eyes flashed with intelligent light as he said, "We say 'Y Gwir Yn Erbyn Y Byd' (Truth against the world). Moreover, you, O Israelite, have uttered the Ineffable Name — 'I AM' — Jh-VH, Jehovah."

The Saint was startled, for here indeed was a link. He was taken 'at the time he was not aware of, and in the manner he was not aware of.'

The Druid continued, "Our ancient Kymric symbol is Awen, or the Holy wings. The three rays or rods of light on our crowns signify the radiating light of Divine intelligence shed upon our Druidic Circle. Another point: we also believe in the Almighty Father. But, Israelite, I am amazed. If God did descend, and dwell on earth as man — whom you declare is one with the Deity, the Almighty Father – then why, believing this, shouldn't men prostrate themselves before Him — if it is proved that He is God. It staggers me, for here are mysteries indeed!"

St. Joseph replied, "There is yet another matter for discussion. Animal sacrifices are world-wide. Can they ransom man, who is superior to the beast? Surely not! We unhesitatingly proclaim God's Son is the one and only Perfect sacrifice the Almighty Father accepts, or ever will acknowledge. Unfortunately, the price was tremendous. To witness it was heart-breaking. The price was His blood shed for remission of sin. His death-bed was a tree; His arms were stretched forth for an unbelieving world.

"The tomb — even death itself — was conquered with the magnificent Life Power that He alone, as God, could display. A soldier pierced His side — but He rose from the grave alive. The same Lord, but, oh, far more wonderful. No barrier kept Him out of our homes. He passed through walls with the same ease as He trod the sky when He left us to return to The Almighty Father of us all."

There was a long pause.

"It is marvelous, Israelite. We also believe that by no other way than by the life of a man is reconciliation with the divine justice of the immortal gods possible. Tell me more, Easterner."

"In the beginning God promised that the seed of woman would defeat evil. A young daughter of Judah, Mary by name, was visited by a heavenly messenger, saying, 'I am Gabriel, who stands in the presence of God, and I am sent to speak to you. You shall conceive and bear a son, and call His name Jesus. He shall be called the Son of the Highest.'

"Oh, Druid brother, here is a profound mystery for you and me. You have mentioned 'Awen' or the 'Holy Wings.' We also have an emblem, a Dove, signifying the great Spirit of God, which overshadowed the maiden chosen for His Mother."

The old Druid rose, and strode to and fro in silence. Then he paused.

"What is the mysterious 'Holy Ghost,' Man of Israel?"

"You have uttered the Name of our Deity! Listen! We choose the most beautiful tree, cut off its side branches and then join two of them to the higher side of the trunk, so that they extend themselves on either side like the arms of a man, making the whole in the shape of a cross. Above, in the bark of the tree, is the word Thaw (Hebrew) by which we mean God. On the right of the arm we inscribe 'Hesus'; on the left, 'Belenus,' on on the trunk, 'Tharamis.' Under this tree we perform the most sacred rites. I would like to share our precious mistletoe or 'All Heal' as our emblem of the Great Healer, who is to appear on the earth at a later day. Our splendid oaks, we believe, represents the Almighty Father, eternal, self-existent, defying all assaults and living eternally; On the oak grows the 'All Heal' Mistletoe, the golden rod or branch. (Homer)

"Is it possible ..." he paused and passed his hand over his forehead — "that Hesus is He whom you call 'Jesus'? I am amazed! What a marvel!"

"I think, Arch Druid," said St. Joseph, "that it will be made plain to you, for He is 'Very God.' "

The Druid was thrilled by the earnest words of his companion:

"I want you to know, Druid, His birth was heralded by a star which outshined the glittering planets. Traveling, it guided the Magi from the shores of the River Euphrates. They came over dry deserts, on swift camels bearing costly gifts to lay in homage at the young King of Israel's feet."

"A star! Wonderful! So this is the explanation to our puzzle. You should know, Easterner, that we have wisdom in these matters, as astronomy has not varied as taught by Pythagoras, and the Greek term for our wise men is 'Saronidae'. It's a small wonder we were unable to explain its appearance or its absence."

"How could you, a Western Student, be as advanced in knowledge as you are, unless our historic records were known to your Order. God entrusted heavenly revelations to our prophets and forefathers, men as frail as ourselves. But they faithfully recorded the Holy One's message. We alone hold the key that explains the hitherto unexplainable."

The sunlight faded. A pale moon appeared and made them realize how the time had flown. At last the Druid wistfully said,

"Everything unknown is doubted."

He turned and faced St. Joseph, and in a slightly aggressive manner, straightened his shoulders, said, "I shall never change!"

St. Joseph said, "There is no need to. We are the expansion. Ponder while I recite a simple narrative. Consider the oaks you love. Have you not felt sorrowful when you saw a proud monarch of the forest fall, its branches smashed, before a high wind?

>I will resist this hateful blast
>I will not bend my proud head, blow, wind,
>It matters not how hard.

"So the Monarch of the woods fell, its pride buried in the soil that nourished it. Suppose for one minute that wind is God's new and better thing for us, to save us from eternal death. Mark this: whenever a super-power or spiritual wind or revelation descends, in whatever form, it demands examination. Otherwise it would be non-existent for you or me. But, if worthy ... what of it? We must weigh 'the Truth' of all new knowledge and not toss it aside, or we may find we are all fools, where others fear not to tread with unshodden feet."

The light faded from the Druid's face as he replied, "Remember, Joseph the merchant, if I do agree in part, I am one of the Tree Arch-Druids of this land, and under obligations to my Order — Druidism will never die."

"Never die! Of course not. It will drape itself in new and wondrous raiment, and arise purified. For in your formula there runs a thread of truth. What is good and true will stand all tests. Only untruth will perish.

"A faith that expands alone bridges space; and it is that which will carry us over to experience and lead us into the courts of knowledge."

He gathered his mantle around him as the evening mists began to rise.

"I will continue to pray to God, Arch-Druid, that the light of revelation may illuminate these mysteries and perhaps some day ..."

"Never, friend. I will ..." His voice trailed off, the last words were never spoken. Stoutly he looked into the solemn earnest eyes fixed so intently on his, as if to draw his secret from him — eyes that had rested on the World's Redeemer — and their mysterious power overwhelmed the Druid. His own eyes sank; he could not, dared not, let himself go.

St. Joseph said, as he laid a hand on his arm, "God will not force you. He won us, and will draw you to Himself some day. But not now ... think about these truths, and perhaps ... Now we must part."

"Yes," said the Druid with a saddened face, "the future is unknown. There is a moaning of sorrow in the wind. I say this — I almost ... wish ... it could be so ... but ... I know not ... listen.

"There are three things by which the conscience binds itself to Truth. The Name of God:

> the rod of him who offers
> up prayers to God;
> the joined right hand."

He held out his hand which St. Joseph gripped and held and in the Druid's noble face came a kindly look as he said, "I will recite for you the most ancient Gorsedd prayer:

"'Grant, O God, Thy Protection;
And in Protection, Strength;
And in Strength, Understanding;
And in Understanding, Knowledge;
And in Knowledge, the Knowledge of Justice;
And in the Knowledge of Justice, the Love of it;
And in that Love, the Love of all Existences;
And in the Love of all Existences, the Love of God.
God and all Goodness.'"

The Arch Druid's eyes, like deep pools, rested on those of his companion.

"Druid brother, may God Almighty bless you and yours, this land, and this people, and unite us all in the true faith. In the name of Jesus — 'Hesus.'"

The Druid turned and walked, deep in thought, through the apple orchard towards his hut. The moonbeams streamed through the leaves on to his white robe, and he was lost in the shadows.

* * * * * * * * * * * * * *

The Druidic teaching concerning a man's spiritual nature:

> "In every person there is a soul
> In every soul there is intelligence
> In every intelligence there is thought
> In every thought there is either good or evil
> In every evil there is death
> In every good there is life
> In every life there is God."

Other Druidic doctrines taught:

"The three foundations of learning: seeing much; studying much; and suffering much."

"The three foundations of judgments: bold design; frequent practice; and frequent mistakes."

"The three foundations of happiness: a suffering with contentment; a hope that it will come; and a belief that it will be."

"The three foundations of thought: perspicuity; amplitude; and preciseness."

"The three qualifications of poetry: endowment of genius; judgment from experience; and happiness of mind."

"The three canons of perspicuity: the word that is necessary; the quantity that is necessary; and the manner that is necessary."

"The three canons of amplitude: appropriate thought; variety of thought; and requisite thought."

The Druidic symbol of the Trinity.

A BRITISH DRUID
DRAWING BY WILLIAM STUKELEY, 1723

CHAPTER V

KING CARADOC OF SILURIA

*"Man
of men at whose strong girdle
hang the Keys of all things."*

"One of the Rulers of choice; one of those brave princes who by reason of their valour could never be overcome save by treachery."

(St. Paul in Britain)

The air was keen with a touch of frost in the fateful year for Siluria, as King Arviragus rode swiftly along the bank of the historic River Usk, and the sun was waking the sleeping world.

The cavalcade had traveled far from Dunmonia. It now rounded "the foot-hills of the interior" through the mist that still veiled much of the beautiful country, rightly named the Tyrol of Britain.

Usk Castle (Usk Castle was probably built much later than the 1st Century) commands a position high above the river. Today it is a picturesque ruin, festooned with ivy.

The massive drum tower was silhouetted against the wooded background. Soaring above the fortress, the stately trees looking like sentinels, protruded above the mist. Noble stags, red deer, and hares, startled at their dewy breakfasts and fled terrified.

The castle-guard anxiously scanned the travellers and were greatly relieved to recognize that Arviragus, King Caradoc's cousin, was the disturber of the early morning hour. The enemy — the Roman legionary headquarters — were but a dozen miles distant.

Oswain, the king's attendant, roused his sleeping monarch who hastily dressed.

A trumpet had summoned the serfs to their various duties.

King Caradoc entered the great banqueting hall and watched the dying embers being fanned into life, wondering what grave turn of events had caused his cousin to seek his advice.

The heavy doors were unbarred in time to admit the panting,

tired horses, which were brought to a sudden halt in the courtyard. The air was misty with the steamy heat of their bodies. The clatter of this unexpected cavalcade in days of war was, to say the least, disturbing.

King Arviragus alone rode into the hall and reined up his charger by the side of his Cousin Caradoc, who stood to receive him.

King Arviragus was a man about middle age, with sons. (His sons are said to have confirmed the gift "Of XII hides" to the Christian settlers.) He gloried in adventures as any boy. He was high-spirited and very handsome and was not above responding to the admiring glances of the ladies. His merry eyes glistened with fun, winning allegiance and devotion. Thus, for the time being, with his anxious relative he swept care aside as he cordially greeted the older man. Caradoc was cheered to hear his ringing laugh, as he related amusing escapes and escapades.

Every hound barked. Dragon, the king's charger, neighed greetings to the strange company of his own pastures. He was tethered to a stable in the hall and not as was the custom to his owner's bed. After a hearty meal the warrior chieftain's brave, keen soldiers in their medieval attire, arranged their war tactics and discussed the best methods to resist the advancing Roman aggression.

Looking back across the centuries, we can but admire them, as we attempt to visualize what these British kings had to face. There were enemy encampments in many places. The enemy appeared above the hills, walking over their farm land, sheltering in their forests. While disloyal native tribes were fostering the enemy, others, as the Silureans and Ordovices, were in open revolt, for Romans were about their homesteads.

Then, too, a great chain of castras, military strongholds, had been erected across our rich land — also beautiful private villas with tesselated pavement and elaborately constructed baths were being erected in the cities and temples for their gods — they meant to stay. Their feet were firmly planted in a land to which they had no manner of claim.

Many years had to run before the British Queen Boadicea,

(or as she was called, Buddig – or Vuddig, delivered her smashing blow. These ocean-cradled isles did not become the crown of victory.

The evening was closing in, King Caradoc rested in his leather-seated chair. A muscular frame bespoke elegance and strength. His tunic was fastened by a belt, and his trousers, loose leggins, were bound to the legs with leather thongs. His Cordovan leather shoes, with gilded clasps attached, were made by his uncle, Manawyddan, who was a "cordwainer."

The great open fireplace was ablaze with flames eating hungrily at the dry branches. Kerns silently moved over the rush floor, casting weird mysterious shadows of grotesque shape. The long oak tables ashine with constant use, were piled high with every available luxury. To the hungry man a well-filled platter and savory cauldron was a goodly sight, and in this hospitable castle there was no lack. Even wheaton cakes made with honey (Excavated in Meare Lake Village, Somerset) were there.

Princess Eurgain, the king's eldest daughter, entered the hall and gave various directions. She was a tall, slender girl, white skinned, and her light tread made little noise as she approached her father, who sat lost in thought, heedless of those around him.

Usk Castle was not their home. The palace was at *Llantwit Major,* where the Channel breezes played around their casement. Usk was a temporary residence, and nearer war activities. He could seldom enjoy more than a few brief hours with his family.

"Our cousin slumbers long," said Princess Eurgain.

The King started; his eyes took in every detail of his frail looking daughter as she stood, the firelight playing on her refined features. She was clad in white heavy woven material, a chain of amber round her neck, her shapely arms encircled with many gold bangles.

Her nut-brown hair fell in waves to her knees, loosely, as was the custom then. She fidgeted uneasily. The king made no answer. His long, sweeping moustache failed to hide a slight sneer which curled round his mouth.

She noted his uncongenial attitude, and her heart failed, for she had a secret to defend. She wondered if any gossip had mentioned her doings.

She ventured another remark:

"Father, I think an escort had better be sent to Ynis Vytren to accompany Grandfather and Gladys. She is young and too beautiful to be unattended in these turbulent days. Here she would be surrounded by our own people."

The king pushed a log into place impatiently.

"Trystan left days ago, according to my instructions. I considered it unwise and unsafe for them, or at least Gladys, to travel at all. However, what you say is true, but Rome hath already found favor with you, and I hear you are courted by Lord Salog, and that you have been with him too much for mere friendliness. Because military duties necessitate his presence in these parts, it becomes the king's daughter to entertain him with courtesy when he is on official duty. But this is no excuse to encourage his attentions. If you can turn from me now, maybe Gladys will do so also."

Eurgain dropped her head and a deep crimson flushed her pale face and neck. So this nightmare moment had at last arrived, and her secret was known to her father. Her lips quivered, and she longed to sink beneath the floor. She licked her dry lips, and then the king asked, "Well what do you say? Is this true?"

"Yes, my father, it is true. We are in love. He would like to ask you for my hand, but he has refrained for the time being until the war is ended."

The king with strained muscles and a voice that thundered, bent towards his daughter, and she felt his hot, quick, angry breath on her cheek.

"Ended! Eurgain! Never! Except with victory to the Islanders and nothing less than complete defeat of our foes. It may not be my lot or privilege to put the enemy to flight, nevertheless, it is inevitable some day." He was silent for a while, and his face softened as his glance fell on her.

"Eurgain, it seems as if an unsheathed sword has fallen

between us; this has hurt me so deeply." His love struggled hard with the scorn he failed to suppress.

Eurgain had a gentle, clinging nature, a character that was easily led by a stronger will than her own. The Princess was by no means lacking in determination, when we learn she faced what to us today, living in religious luxury, would be an amazing and soul-terrorizing ordeal — martyrdom.

The wood in the great fireplace crackled. Eurgain's eyes were swimming in tears. At last the king said, "I am not one to be needlessly cruel, my child, as you know, but it is a bitter blow. I have other pressing duties and romance finds little leisure in my soldier's life. These are critical days. It is this which has brought our cousin here from Dunmonia to consult me. I think you have forfeited the right to be present at this meeting."

The hall was filled with a rush of wind and quick footsteps. It was Lleyn, the king's youngest son, who entered. A bright smile beamed upon his sunny face, and a whiff of the sweet heather uplands pervaded the hall.

He was a sportsman, every inch of him, fleet of foot, and an expert where others failed to catch and land the best salmon. His eyes glistened as he held up a magnificent one. He advanced.

"Isn't it a beauty father? But why these tables full of food?" His eyes swept over the extra dainties. "Perhaps it's a feast. Why do you leave us? You just arrived a few hours ago."

"War, Lleyn, and all it means creeps into castles or hovels. Your worthy cousin, Arviragus, sleeps. he needed my advice, and after this feast they leave at sundown. He received certain news from Verulum that Vespasian, aided by his son Titus (Both of these Roman soldiers came from Spain, and later become emperors of Rome) is casting longing eyes towards Cambria and Dunmonia. We have decided to stop this by concentrating troops on the Brendon Hills. Nearby there is a suitable spot at Bishop Lydeard, namely Conquest Farm. The rounded hills thereabout will afford good shelter for our troops and horses, because Platius has fixed a camp between Silbury Hill and Amesbury. Vespasian and Titus, his son, I hear, are at Hampden Hill, near Ilchester, with a strong force."

"I have promised to dispatch a trusted messenger to him; perhaps he is overwhelmed. Then we think it would be best for him to retreat to the west, towards Caer Wyse (Exeter) in case of need. You know Roman castras (camps) stretch across our land. It is a strong line of defense which we dare not ignore — and their legionary bases are full of fighting soldiers. We can only guess why Caesar sends his best generals. I guess this nut is the hardest they have ever pressed their teeth on.

"Another thing — I hear Ostorious Scapula is extra alert. I do not trust that man, in or out of my sight, and he will stop at nothing so long as his own skin is not scratched, but wants victory at another's expense. His methods are low down. He is most unscrupulous, not a brave, clean fighter, and besides, he is an arrogant coward. Bah! He thinks a prick of our swords will be the finish. Well, I am not over keen to soil mine. I would gladly leave that privilege for others, and use mine on a worthier foe."

"I leave early tomorrow for Caer Essylt, and Arviragus should be far south when the night shadows fall."

"But mark this — I cannot, dare not, minimize the extremely dangerous position we are faced with. Not only the Iceni, but the Brigantes in the north, under the spell of influencial Romans, have formed strong alliances with our mutual enemy. To look for assistance from them is sheer folly. Had they stood beside me shoulder to shoulder in a national cause, surely we would have won. We are out to protect what we love and would willingly die for. They desire only extra land and power.

"Then, Lleyn, there is your Uncle Aulus Plautius. Although he married my sister, he does not love our cause. He is a full-fledged Roman, and as bitter a foe as any of the other generals. I am a fly in his honey-pot." His foot beat the scrunchy reeds impatiently, and his voice became hard and rasping, and with a quivering finger he pointed at Eurgain.

"It seems to be the fashion for my family to form marriage ties with Romans. These foreigners not only grab at land, but would carry away our daughters!"

Sweat broke out on his face and ran in little rivers on his puckered brow.

"It is strange that arrows from home bows should penetrate the deepest and ache the worst. What I feel is that seven long years of ceaseless struggle, mental strain, and physical weariness, is poorly rewarded."

His voice trailed off to a weary moan. He seized a mead flagon and quaffed the contents at a gulp. Around his eyes gathered the deep shade of fatigue. Leon stretched his long body, and wagging his tail, licked the king's hand.

"No, Leon, lie down! Lleyn, if it were not that there are greater ideals for our native country, I should be inclined to retire in favor of Arviragus, or someone else. But it would be like the captain of an argosy in distress, to swim and save his life and care little for his drowning crew."

He stooped and picking up a blazing log, flung it savagely on to the flames.

"Like Pendragon I must carry on. After all, even if I fail, I shall have done my best, and if need be shall fulfill to the letter our Triad and die for my country."

Eurgain listened with mixed emotions. Never before had she realized her father's difficulties. He had thundered out her name in the bitterness of his heart. She felt paralyzed, ashamed and so involved, yet she was incapable of alleviating his pain.

Lleyn, always ready to help others, said: "Father, though you leave us shortly, and we never know whether you will be spared to return, I beg of you let not this fresh trial estrange us all. Do not let us break home ties. Eurgain may need a home, and she is one of us, even if a love for an enemy has grown. I ask a great heart sacrifice of you, my father, for all our sakes.

"Father, listen. Lord Salog is a very noble fellow; he has been most anxious to meet you and explain. I have good cause to know how kind he is. He implored me just now to make it possible for him to approach you about my sister, and that if I had your consent I was to call him here by three blasts from my horn from the turret."

"Carry out this plan, Lleyn. If the love affair has reached this point, it is best to place love in right position, for others besides ourselves know. For Eurgain's sake we had better settle it."

Lleyn brushed his sister's hair with his lips as he passed her. Eurgain sat petrified, and heard the long musical notes echoing up and up in the woods, while the king strode to and fro, lost in thought.

With wonderful instinct, Leon laid his head on her knee, and lifting one paw, gazed out of his intelligent and gentle eyes at his young mistress. Eurgain was comforted, her tears trickled perilously near his eyes.

Then they entered, her brother coming first. We will leave them to their discussion and explanation. King Caradoc, a brilliant leader of men, a hard fighter, had beneath his tunic a very tender heart, being so beloved because of his great understanding of those around him. Because of this he suffered as such natures do.

Suddenly the middens doors were flung open and the hall was filled with the aroma of smoking cauldrons, venison, roast boar, and other choice viands. Mead was in the "Hirlas horns" embossed with silver. Lord Salog refused to partake of the feast, and it was better so.

The lovers shyly threaded their way through the castle kerns, perspiring cooks and retainers, together with the men-at-arms, a merry crew. Knowing winks followed the nervous lover. He would have preferred a battle any day to hearing the taunting remarks which followed them as they left the hall.

Dragon strained towards his young mistress, impatiently snuffing round her for an apple. She stroked his great neck and kissed his silky nose.

"Oh, Salog, suppose father does not return. From what you have told me my heart is heavy—war is so cruel!" She could say no more for the choking in her throat.

Salog drew her towards him and lifted her face to his, and she saw a great love shining there. With pitiful little smiles, they silently embraced. Then he mounted his horse, rode down the wooded slopes and was lost to view.

CHAPTER VI

"THE DOMUS DEI"

*"In every person there is a soul;
In every soul there is intelligence;
In every intelligence there is thought;
In every thought there is either good or evil;
In every evil there is death;
In every good there is life;
In every life there is God."*

Druidic Teaching.

Eighteen years after the Crucifixion, a crisis was approaching which was to affect war conditions in Britain, much to the discredit of the Italian rulers and their mean and powerful accomplice, Queen Cartismandua.

IN "SUMMERLAND"

On the dizzy height of "The Holy Hill," or Gorsedd Mound today called Glastonbury Tor, the Arch Druid Bran stood alone. A Druidic assembly had just broken up, yet the benign old Welshman lingered in that isolated spot between heaven and earth, where the unhindered breeze swayed his vestments.

On all sides space. A spot where the firmament seemed to embrace this majestic height so beloved by generations resembling in its formation a gigantic cone. Have we finished with romance? Is there still a future, brighter by far than the past for this lonely monarch of the ancients? Many think so.

He gazed into the evening sky, bathed in sunset splendor. The great sun, the winged globe, so reverenced by the Egyptian mystics, was being veiled in clouds. He could just see the channel waters that lay between him and Cambria.

His eyes followed the retreating forms of the Bards — "wearers of the long blue robes" — the Ovates having a place in the assembly with their robes of bright green, and the Druids as the —

"Splendid race wearers of
gold chains — the eminently white."

"Prehistoric London." Gordon.

One head after another sank from view as they threaded their way over the soft turf to their homesteads in the meadowland. Wistfully he watched them. Did he foresee changes? A troubled thought made him frown.

At the base of the hill stood a primitive building, called by some "Ecclesia Vistua." It was the first Christian sanctuary ever erected in Britain, constructed of wattles, withies, or osiers, bound with daub, as used by the Lake folk, who entwined them round tree poles which supported their roofs. (Vide Lake Village at Meare, excavated by Bulleigh, 1930.)

He noted with interest how the Easterners erected their huts round about, as if to guard "The Secret of the Lord." (The wattle church that Christ built in his youth at Glastonbury.)

What was the mystery, we wonder?

Wild speculations are still unanswered and the treasured secrets are still enfolded. Above, the winds sport with the leafy guardians, whose roots, like the tender fingers of love, cling round the tired bodies of innumerable saints.

The wise old Druid questioned the advisability of his nephew Arviragus, who had granted "twelve hides" of land to these foreigners. It rankled in his heart.

St. Joseph the merchant had, after eighteen years, greeted him warmly on his arrival at Avalon.

The question of rival religions suddenly confronted him. Horrified, he discovered that neither the attraction nor interest in this man had died. Vividly he recalled their conversation. Foolishly he had followed the missionaries into their sacred enclosure, where their customs or ritual had been explained. He was sensitive to supernatural influences, and he met it there. It seemed to cling to him as officiated on "The Holy Hill." His curiosity was being severely punished. As he leaned against the monolith, was it his fancy that he beheld a flash across the heavens? In an awestruck voice he murmured:

"The holy Awen? Rays? or is it the Christian's Holy Bird? Am I mad ... am I a Christian at heart and a Druid by profession? It's conflicting, the old and the known — the new and the unknown."

How long he remained transfixed he never knew — until his soul poised and planed down to earthly conditions.

"No, I cannot; I must consider Druidic and national distress and not add to difficulties. It would disturb the entire fabric of our Order at a time when our country is in pain to be delivered of a national foe."

He wrestled alone, taking his will to task with all the strength of his strong character, stiffening his soul's longing with cherished memories, smothering his conscience against the Infinite One, formerly veiled in flesh.

Painful circumstances were surely and stealthily closing in around his life. For a cloud of sorrow with a lining of light was due to enfold this noble man who would capitulate to the world's Redeemer.

It is good for us, too, to face difficulties and to suffer, too, for what ultimately becomes our most cherished possession. We are born into the Christian fold as inheritors of a grand faith. We amble as lambs beside their fat mothers, and graze in the sweet pastoral grass. We take it all for granted, as a rule, and that is perhaps why we value our religious privileges so little. Others, and even ourselves some day, may question our inheritance. Let us ask ourselves which lambs will value it most?

King Caradoc's youngest daughter, Gladys, had accompanied her grandfather to Avalon on a visit. She decided to go up the hill to meet him, as he seemed unusually long. At last she reached the summit and beheld him silhouetted against the vivid colors of the sunset sky.

The sun's last rays were reflected from his crown and breastplate, and it made her catch her breath, for the Druidic regalia is very gorgeous.

At sixteen years of age she was, as to personal attraction, what she was by birth: a high-born maiden, whose genealogy was pure and unbroken, or her grandfather could never have become Arch Druid. In spite of her coarse homespun robe bound to her trim figure by a leather girdle, she was every inch a princess. There was little to depict her rank except, perhaps, a gold torque and heavy arm bracelets.

Her chief beauty lay in her large, gentle eyes and her magnificent auburn hair, like burnished copper. On her feet she wore Cordovan leather sandals.

The Arch-Druid beheld her, and a wave of affection swept through him.

"Gladys, why have you sought me here?"

"Forgive me, grandfather, but I feel so restless, for Trystan had brought home tidings — all seems sad there now; I wish I had remained at home. I fear things are none too bright and who knows?" she said, sadly looking at him.

Bran gazed in admiration at her troubled face and laid his hand on her shoulder. She was blossoming into a beautiful and intellectual woman, and he feared for her future, for Roman officers were posted over much of Britain and many homes were drenched in sorrow.

"Look, child, at that gorgeous sunset. You are beautiful and in these days, it will be a dangerous possession. Keep the memory of this evening in your heart, your body chaste, and your soul as the fragrant flowers. Come, let us descend, for I am hungry, and the sun no longer shines for us."

Skipping beside him down the deep gully, she related home news, and her bright laugh echoed up the rocks.

"What do you think? Trystan has brought venison for us, and maybe it is already in the cookpot."

The education of the Silurian nobility took place at Caerleon and it seems to have been extremely efficient, if one can judge by the famous speech King Caradoc made in Rome. Undoubtedly, the young princesses were well educated, too, and we have some good proof of this. Gladys was soon to be uprooted — transplanted into Italy, to become famous, as wife of a nobleman, a hymn-writer and, lastly, hostess to the Great Apostles.

The bodyguard of picked men were delayed, and Trystan stoutly resisted their desire to leave, unattended except for his presence, saying it was the king's wish, and the journey was dangerous. It was surely no chance that caused them to tarry awhile.

The elderly men were drawn into friendly talk over the peat fires which Gladys kindled as she spun the fleecy wool. The ever burning discussions on faith were thrashed out, which to the sensitive girl became a soul stirring experience.

Many a night she gazed into the star-spangled heavens, longing to stifle the desire to believe and be at rest in her soul.

Then, one never-to-be-forgotten day she joined the villagers and went into the Christian sanctuary. When they knelt, she knelt, too, on her shaking knees. For what was she doing there?

Nearly two thousand years ago, she faced a change of belief. We know from her history, which will meet us further on, how brilliant a woman she became.

One day she called Leon and sought the streamlet that gushed out of "The Holy Hill," flying from what? Some power that was to prove her salvation.

She seated herself beside the crystal water which flows abundantly and ceaselessly, spraying rocks and ferns. Who has solved the mystery of its source, a gift of the Creator? Lost in meditation — suddenly her soul was born. All doubt fled. The light breeze lifted her curls and a rush of tears relieved her soul agony. The struggle was ended — she was a Christian.

Toiling up the hill was St. Joseph of Arimathea, and he suddenly stopped as he perceived her, breaking a twig as he turned to go. She looked up, and rose and pleaded with him to remain, smiling through her tears; and he wondered.

"I sought this spot, my child, to think awhile, but did not intend to disturb you. It was the twig's fault."

"Nay, Father Joseph, I have much to say to you," and she timidly touched his hand, and with shining eyes said, "I believe Jesus is the Christ, the Son of the living God. I desire to be baptized before I leave for home. Will you do this for me?"

The light wind rustled through the trees, and he looked at the lovely girl, her hands clasped, her eyes searching his so eloquently for his consent.

"Dear daughter, do you realize that baptism is a covenant God will consider binding and unbreakable? Perhaps you may have to suffer as some are doing now in Roman amphitheatres. What of it, if you should be called to witness, at the cost of life itself — and what of martyrdom? Remember this is a covenant beyond this life and the grave."

"I have considered — I am willing to risk all for Him. In this matter I consider I am free to choose, however difficult the future may be. Communicating with my father is extremely difficult, as he may be away north."

"Then, my child, God willing, you shall have your request. Watch and pray and seek me tomorrow, and we will have talk further. Ponder well — and God guide thee."

On reaching the village she found everyone excited, for their escort had arrived, travel stained and weary — specially chosen for their devotion and loyalty to the royal household.

A few days later, when dawn was breaking over the hills, flooding the misty valleys with soft light, the young princess, accompanied by a small gathering of Christian friends, proceeded silently to the appointed spot for her baptismal rites.

By her side walked her grandfather, her only relative, who glanced at her nervously. He had ceased to try and turn her. She grasped his hand, led him along whispering: "You, too, will become a Christian." She felt his hand quiver.

He feared as to the future, and how it would separate her from all the traditions of her people, and what he so valued. He was on a mental rack and suffering acutely; and, if he but knew, it was the faint light of a new morn pouring light into every recess of his darkness. The heavenly beams were surging over the hills of his difficulties with irresistible stealth. But he had a fighting spirit — and strong character. He watched with heart-longing the tall disciple of the lord perform the wonderful rite. He heard the few and solemn words as she sealed her faith in living water, the drops of which rested in the waves of her thick hair and caught the sunlight, scintillating like jewels.

Gladys knelt, and, pausing a moment, Bran knelt beside her as St. Joseph's hands rested on her bowed head.

"The Lord bless you and keep you; the Lord lift up the light of His countenance upon you and give you peace, now and forevermore. Amen.

"Let us depart in peace."

Gladys rose, eyes filled with tears; St. Joseph stooped and kissed her forehead. She raised his hand to her lips, turned away, mute and overwhelmed.

From our old books I know that Joseph came of old to Glastonbury, and there the heathen Prince Arviragus gave him an isle of marsh on which to build.

"And there he built with wattles from the marsh
A little lonely church in days of yore.
The cup, the cup itself from which our Lord
Drank at the last sad supper with his own
Arimathaean Joseph journeying brought
To Glastonbury, where the thorn
Blossoms at Christmas, mindful of our Lord."
Tennyson.

A LEGEND OF GLASTONBURY

"Who hath not hir'd of Avalon?
Twas talk'd of much and long agon: —
The wonders of the Holy Thorn,
The which, zoon ater Christ was born,
Here a planted war by Arimathe,
Thie Joseph that com'd over sea,
And planted Christianity.
Tha za that whun a landed vust,
(Zich plazen was in God's own trust)
A stuck his staff into the groun,
And over his shoulder lookin roun,
Whativer mid his lot bevall,
He cried aloud now, 'weary all!'
The staff het budded and het grew,
And at Christmas bloom'd the whol da droo,
And still het blooms at Christmas bright,
But best tha za at dork midnight."

Written in the Somerset dialect of A.D. 1870
from oral traditions prevalent in Glastonbury

silently to the appointed spot for her baptismal rites.

By her side walked her grandfather, her only relative, who glanced at her nervously. He had ceased to try and turn her. She grasped his hand, led him along whispering: "You, too, will become a Christian." She felt his hand quiver.

He feared as to the future, and how it would separate her from all the traditions of her people, and what he so valued. He was on a mental rack and suffering acutely; and, if he but knew, it was the faint light of a new morn pouring light into every recess of his darkness. The heavenly beams were surging over the hills of his difficulties with irresistible stealth. But he had a fighting spirit — and strong character. He watched with heart-longing the tall disciple of the lord perform the wonderful rite. He heard the few and solemn words as she sealed her faith in living water, the drops of which rested in the waves of her thick hair and caught the sunlight, scintillating like jewels.

Gladys knelt, and, pausing a moment, Bran knelt beside her as St. Joseph's hands rested on her bowed head.

"The Lord bless you and keep you; the Lord lift up the light of His countenance upon you and give you peace, now and forevermore. Amen.

"Let us depart in peace."

Gladys rose, eyes filled with tears; St. Joseph stooped and kissed her forehead. She raised his hand to her lips, turned away, mute and overwhelmed.

From our old books I know that Joseph came of old to Glastonbury, and there the heathen Prince Arviragus gave him an isle of marsh on which to build.

"And there he built with wattles from the marsh
A little lonely church in days of yore.
The cup, the cup itself from which our Lord
Drank at the last sad supper with his own
Arimathaean Joseph journeying brought
To Glastonbury, where the thorn
Blossoms at Christmas, mindful of our Lord."
Tennyson.

A LEGEND OF GLASTONBURY

*"Who hath not hir'd of Avalon?
Twas talk'd of much and long agon: —
The wonders of the Holy Thorn,
The which, zoon ater Christ was born,
Here a planted war by Arimathe,
Thie Joseph that com'd over sea,
And planted Christianity.
Tha za that whun a landed vust,
(Zich plazen was in God's own trust)
A stuck his staff into the groun,
And over his shoulder lookin roun,
Whativer mid his lot bevall,
He cried aloud now, 'weary all!'
The staff het budded and het grew,
And at Christmas bloom'd the whol da droo,
And still het blooms at Christmas bright,
But best tha za at dork midnight."*

Written in the Somerset dialect of A.D. 1870
from oral traditions prevalent in Glastonbury

CHAPTER VII

QUEEN AREGWEDD *(Cartismandua)*

The sun beat fiercely on a castle in the north of England, the home and military center of the queen of the Brigantes. She was great niece of the infamous traitor in the Julian war — Mandubratius — or Avary. She and her father kept green the family reputation of vice.

In one of the turrets of the castle there was a chamber, much used by this clever and scheming woman. Today she awaited the arrival of a Roman general, having selected this particular retreat on account of its privacy. Its only approach was by a single stairway.

In a fever of expectancy she restlessly paced to and fro over a handsome Persian rug. The summer heat was choked with the Oriental perfumes she used. She frequently paused before the open casement, eagerly searching the wooded hills, the sunlight firing the copper tints in the waves of her glossy hair like a raven's wing, which was coiled into a knot, into which she had pinned a crimson rose. She towered above most men, erect and every inch a queen; her firmly-moulded limbs were perfect, above which she turned her proud head.

Handsome, steel–blue eyes, cold and hard, flashed restlessly beneath her broad forehead. Men were entranced, and soon fell under her magnetic attractions and influence. But it was admiration dearly bought, if the acquaintance ripened into friendship, for she scrupled not to extract the most out of the lesser personalities about her, who scarcely realized that they were being drawn into a veritable spider's web of intrigue. No wonder she was loathed by her own sex, who feared and suffered in silence. Women, to this British Amazon, were too insignificant to be considered. She was a treacherous woman. Thus her character has drifted down the centuries to us. Let us imagine she possessed virtues which are unrecorded.

She hovered near a cabinet, and from time to time drew forth a long parchment roll. It was not valuable because it was vellum, nor because it had been presented to her by one of her devotees from Italy. Nay, its value lay in the message she had laboriously inscribed thereon.

She was conniving to checkmate her hated relative, King Caradoc. He was too much of a national hero, too straight and clean a fighter, too honorable to please her. He acted as an irritant. His nobility and amazing powers of organization as Pendragon acted unpleasantly, as a silent menace and reproof. "Hateful man" she muttered.

Alliance with a national foe was what she schemed, and she left no stone unturned to dethrone him.

The king's ideal was for the islanders to stand and unite in keeping a common foe at arm's length, and if possible to drive them far away.

This did not fit in with her ideas at all. She was too deeply involved in sacrificing her blood brothers for her own personal ambitions.

"No, it's unthinkable! What better friends than those splendid and wealthy warriors? As for Caradoc, I care nothing."

Rome had cast its spell over her; its luxuries had penetrated her northern home, and Romans she adored. Today she watched for her latest fancy, General Ostorius Scapula, to whom she had sent an imperative summons, desiring him to hold converse with her as soon as possible, with injunctions to spare neither rider nor steed. She imagined she was desperately in love with him, and a hundred times she pictured his graceful mantle flowing over his shining armour, and the fluttering feathers in his helmet. Having enthroned him in her heart, she intended to give him the privilege of carrying out her treacherous schemes.

"If he does not come soon," she said, "I shall push these hated walls down; I am in a fever of expectation. Why is he overdue? I hate to be kept waiting."

Leaning out once again, she beheld what she had wearily waited for, a tiny cloud of dust seen here and there along the wooded path little noticed and off the beaten track, but frequently used by her secret agents.

"He comes, my adored hero."

She pressed a rose she wore to her heart, until its beautiful head snapped off and fell at her feet. She flung it far out into the courtyard angrily, and in her haste to remove what remained, she pricked her finger.

"I suppose I deserve to be punished. True; I have deposed my hated husband, who is a spoon-fed babe beside this Roman giant. Bah!"

General Ostorius Scapula rode fast, and skillfully brought his charger to a halt in the courtyard of the castle. He was told to mount the steps, as the queen expected him.

She had seen him arrive on his foam-flecked steed, and listened excitedly for the clanking of his armor and heavy footsteps. Now they were approaching near the door, so she posed gracefully on a divan.

"Madam, am I permitted to enter?" said a soft voice.

"Enter, General Scapula. I have begrudged the minutes that will curtail our discussions."

He beheld the queen languidly fanning herself. She graciously extended her jewelled hand, over which he bent low.

He was a powerfully-built man. Large eyes looking out through heavily lashed lids were his redeeming feature in otherwise poor features. But they were shifty eyes — untrustworthy, roaming eyes, noting everything.

He furtively glanced at his dictatoress. He measured the cunning woman who sent him such authoritative messages. Was he not Caesar's servant? One monarch was enough, surely? But he knew what a refusal to carry out her scheme might mean. They were a well-matched and greatly feared pair when evil was taking its walks abroad.

He admired her beauty, but she was his great fear; and because he couldn't overcome this he loathed her. He would have rejoiced to know some sword had done its work. With those feelings in his heart, he bent before her in the suave and courtly manner of his native land.

Queen Cartismandua, he was sure, intended him to carry out some inglorious deed; moreover, he knew she would not hesitate to see he carried it out thoroughly. She was as much a tyrant as Caesar Claudius himself, or any other emperor.

Moreover, if he failed or perhaps was exposed, she would revel in the thought that, at any rate, her part was screened.

Like most men, he was flattered that she admired him. Watching her every movement, he thought, "Does she like my feathers, or my armor? Queen or no queen, my time will come, fair Signora. I will pay you back with interest, and such an alluring bait is mine ! Ha!"

He spoke aloud, "Sovereign of the Brigantes, fairest rose of Britain, behold me! I have hurried here as you had bidden. I hunger, I thirst. I am weary and hot. My horse is half dead. I spared neither man nor beast. For what purpose? From your messenger I learned it was an urgent and private matter."

She glanced up at his splendid strength, for he had remained standing, helmet in hand, before her. The sunlight was reflected from his armor and lit up the dark walls of the chamber. She rose slowly with a scornful and offended air.

"Alla gracia!" he murmured to himself. "What's wrong now?" He hated her all the more in this perfumed atmosphere from which he would gladly have fled.

"Poor fly; I am in her web. Another victim of her ..." He started, for somehow she had drawn nearer him.

"You haven't asked about my health. Have you ceased to be interested in me, and would you cease to be called my friend? Remember, Ostorius, if you are not a friend you are an enemy — I don't know of any other way. Remember," she said, her jewelled finger pointing to the floor, "that within these solid foundations are cheerless chambers. Is this your greeting to a queen of foreign race who has, alas, let deeper sentiments grow?" She leaned toward him. Her hot passionate breath held him spellbound. This human, beautiful woman, with no moral code, had been surrounded by every influence of low ideals since childhood.

"Perhaps," she breathed, fiercely angry, "our northern climate has cooled the fires of interest, or deeper sentiments?"

He blanched beneath her threats. For they were not empty threats, he felt sure, as many an aggressor before had discovered too late to escape imprisonment. He bit his lips.

Eagerly he followed her movements as she glided over the rich rugs, her eyes ablaze with fury. As a snake, he held himself ready, watching his quarry, but never flinched, for he knew it would be the end. Will against will, hate against hate. Which would win?

He felt as if he had had a cold shower after his hot ride, and he shivered.

"I know," she said, "that military matters are urgent, but you did not ask about my well-being! I hesitate now, wondering if I can trust you with this delicate mission that requires secrecy and skill. There are others devoted to our interests, for aren't Rome's interests mine also — namely, the ending of this war?

"Forgive me, your Majesty. Indeed, I never intended to think lightly of any favor which you are gracious enough to bestow. I am always your sincere admirer and devoted servant; ready when Caesar's work permits, to perform any mission Your Majesty may wish accomplished."

"Admirer! Servant! — A noble banquet for a starving heart. I seek no menial homage or servitude! I want an equal! a friend!.. A ..I'm slighted – hurt and my — oh! enough.""Madam, who could equal you in beauty, or rank, let alone power!"

"Stop this parrying with words, Ostorius. Let's get down to business now, and to what affects our joint interests ... Caradoc!"

She moved to the casement, slowly opened a drawer, and drew out her precious document. She looked superb. Fascinated, he watched her slender fingers close over the roll.

"Kindly remember all details which I want accomplished. I have a letter which must be placed in the hand of Caradoc when he is captured or so sorely pressed by your army as to need assistance. Of course, imprisonment is the only solution that will speedily work satisfactorily for all parties. I want him as my prisoner first. Then I will hand him over to Caesar, if Caradoc consents to accept my hospitality, that's fine. Let him feel free, but be careful that there is no loophole in the plans by which he might escape. Rebellion is to be encouraged; see to it! Aulus Plautius does not count relationships, but is out to work with us, and Vespasian is preparing to march westward to Dunmonia. You had better concentrate around the Caradoc Hills. 'Caer Essylt' is a good position. Entice his army there. We must frustrate any fresh move from Cambria."

"Madam, your words stir up feelings of homesickness that are hard to curb." The queen laid her hand on his arm, and leaning toward him, her beautiful eyes gleaming, whispered fiercely, "Think, my friend, what a big reward Claudius would confer upon you, if such a triumph crowns your military career.

"Think what a spectacular procession Rome would witness, if Caradoc walked beside your charger!"

Their hands met in a grip that spelled doom for a brave British hero.

"Think!" she whispered, glancing anxiously at the door, Caradoc in chains. I think I will follow you, and perhaps I, too, might claim my share of the spoils.

"I've heard that you have a spacious villa. Couldn't you lend it to a queen?"

"Your majesty would be suitably housed here; it is at your service." A sneer curled around his cruel mouth.

"Remember this, Ostorius," she continued breathlessly, his evil eyes glistening as they met hers. "Now is your greatest opportunity. Seize Caradoc and bring him here *as my guest.* In this invitation I offer him protection and cordial hospitality as a neighbor in distress. Under my protection he will be safely housed, and most welcome."

The traitoress lowered her voice still more; "I did not add that his bed would be straw, and that his bangles would be iron manacles. They are already prepared to adorn his sinewy arms ... They must be *so weary* of swinging his sword, and even arms need repose, Oh Ostorius!"

"Madam, you are wonderful!" And a gleam of genuine admiration lit up his face — her only reward!"

"I will do my best to assist you to carry out our joint plan, by fair means or — or — in whatever way I can. If I fail, may my bleeding heart be laid at your feet, and spurned as I would deserve." With a touch of ironic pleasure he added, bowing low, "And as I greatly desire to behold a beautiful girl of my acquaintance to whom I am engaged, I will certainly try to send King Caradoc instead. Should you visit our splendid city of Rome, my wife, which she will be by then, will assuredly do her best to make your visit pleasurable!" Before rising fires of hate had time to explode, he had bowed himself from her presence.

Bronze head of Claudius possibly from a statue of the Emperor on horseback (height 12 in, 31 cm), date about AD 46. The eye sockets were probably inlaid with glass.

CHAPTER VIII

SENATOR AULUS RUFUS PUDENS PUDENTIUS

Cambria is a land of romance; a land whose lofty mountains soar to majestic heights, out of whose sides beautiful waterfalls thunder and cascade through narrow ravines, over huge boulders, meandering through grassy meadows to a nuptial ceremonial with the Channel waters.

Mother Nature has guarded the secret of bygone ages well; of her sons and daughters, their primitive weapons, cook-pots and funeral vases; while the monolithic wonders stand on the purple carpeted hills, testifying in silence to a faith that was worth toiling for.

We would be poorer to forget historical and legendary tales which cling to the ivy-festooned walls of their ancient fortresses; in many cases rebuilt on the ruins of still older homes whose chieftains were kings of their own castles, their turrets fashioned to bristle with arrows.

The Avalon travellers were nearing Usk castle, temporary home of King Caradoc, when one of their horses fell so lame they were held up not far from a Roman encampment, and were seen by a Roman officer who was patrolling his district. Seeing their difficulties, he dispatched a soldier to help. This breakdown necessitated their seeking shelter at a wayside "hospice." (From the Latin word "hospitium.") It chanced that the good dame knew who they were, and was overjoyed at the accident, for did not some of her own royal relatives require her assistance?

It was a proud moment indeed. Her portly form swung around, Martha-like, amidst her shining pots and pans, and she laid out apples, thick cream and filled her best Hirlas horn with mead for the Arch Druid.

She gathered her choicest flowers for the daughter of her king, apologizing proudly for the absence of her brave man; for was he not fighting for the king?

After the ample fare, they sat outside the creeper covered homestead, enjoying the sunshine. The weary Druid slumbered. Gladys took little notice of the Roman military movements. She lived in the atmosphere of war.

The time passed quickly as she rested. Lost in a reverie, her mind travelled back to her Avalon visit. She clung to it as something to be held within, much as an unborn infant is guarded by the mother.

Threading his way over the rough path, advanced fate. Until his shadow lengthened in the dust and a young Roman officer paused before her uncertainly, she did not notice him.

She started violently, filled with surprise. Alarm glinted beneath sweeping lashes. An awkward pause. He bowed low, and she rose and slightly inclined her head.

"May I address myself to you, fair lady, since my soldier has obtained a horse for your group?" She extended her hand.

"Sir, be seated; we are most grateful indeed, for we truly desire to reach home before nightfall."

Seated beside her, he couldn't help but admire the quiet girl with the most glorious hair he had ever seen, and her deep steadfast eyes bewildered him. What struck him most was her quiet, dignified manner. Holding her bouquet of roses, slowly she detached a bud and held it towards him.

"Will you accept this? It is all I have to offer for your great courtesy to us in this untimely breakdown and I know horses are scarce these days."

He took it. "It is like a breath of home. Many like it grow on my arcade at Castello Samnium where many farmers work on my land. I am not a regular soldier, but was forced to join Caesar's army unwillingly. I don't love these chilly isles, although I own a villa at Regnum."

She looked surprised and remarked, "I hear your people have built a great city at Uriconium (Chichester) with a forum, streets, and baths on British soil! Are you staying here?"

"No! I have recently arrived, sent here by Aulus Palutius Practor Castrorum, at Regnum."

Gladys started, and became horribly suspicious, and finally blurted out, "He married King Caradoc's sister, Pomponia Graecina. He is a bitter foe to this Isle," and in a gentler tone she added, "I wish you were under any other general."

"War, fair lady, is an exacting taskmaster; it doesn't care about flesh and blood, love or sorrow, birth or death. Let me introduce myself; I am Senator Pudens Pudentius; I have had little to do with any woman outside my own home. And now, alas, it is empty, for my spendid mother, stately as any queen, has died since I left Italy and I am very lonely."

She looked at him sympathetically. He lowered his voice.

"I'm not joking," he said earnestly, "when I tell you that never before have I spoken with any woman with greater pleasure than this short time with you." He touched her arm. "Listen, for you may need a friend in the enemy's camp, and war is uncertain. Will you — can you — trust me, a stranger?"

She looked wistfully away towards the hills, for his rich musical voice, with a timbre strangely delightful to her sensitive ear — quite different from the harsh Welsh voices — had suddenly ceased.

"I would like to trust you, Senator, and somehow — I feel I can, but — it is — difficult — to say yes."

"You have answered; all is well," he said with a bright smile, and as they talked, she felt increasing interest and attraction towards this enemy of her nation, pleading so earnestly to be believed; and she read, too, his unmistaken admiration. Suddenly a great nervousness overwhelmed her and a faint color suffused her cheek.

Their horses were being led forward. "Oh," he thought, "how can I prolong this hour?"

As she watched the preparations, his quick eye noted her noble bearing, her gold ornaments — what was she called, he wondered.

He was not lacking in personal attractions, and had a noble bearing, finely-shaped limbs, and, in the picturesque uniform of Caesar's army, was a marked man, with Greek features and thick wavy hair.

"They are ready too quickly!" he remarked, searching her fair face, that was to leave only a memory — a mental portrait.

She turned toward him and met his look. A love was born, the future of all unknown held in the balance, and noble lives to become stars in an immortal crown was the result of this sudden welding of hearts and souls. The affinity of souls which drew these two together alone will bear the strain of life's trials. It came to stay between a British girl of royal birth and a Roman nobleman.

The tension ended as a quick sigh escaped her lips and she buried her head in the flowers, lest he should see her secret.

"We, I hope, are friends, Senator Pudens, are we not?"

"No, more," he replied, as he raised her bud to his lips. "May I ask your name?"

"Why not?" she replied brightly. "It is no secret. My name is Gladys; I am the youngest daughter of King Caradoc of Siluria."

She became alarmed as she saw him turn deadly white, and he swayed. For he felt as if all hope had had its death-blow; that this sweet woman could never be his. He passed his hand over his face, moist with sudden distress and, bowing stiffly, prepared to leave her.

"No, Senator Pudens, do not leave me this way, because you have learned I am of royal birth. I cannot help being a northern maid, nor you a Roman nobleman. We are beholden to you for your kindness. See, Trystan leads a fresh horse, and now," she said wistfully, "we must part and each go our own way,"

"Princess Gladys, I shall never forget you, whatever your rank, nor this short time spent here."

He breathed hard, as one gasping for breath, as he bent towards her and murmured, "You are my ideal woman — a maid — and soon, maybe some Britisher will win your love. I shall envy that man and wherever you are I shall know. Forgive, I pray, this presumption."

The hot color glowed in her face, enhancing its beauty. She felt herself becoming more and more involved, for he seemed to compel her attention.

"I speak from my heart," he said gravely. "Should you ever think of me, remember, although I am of a foreign nation, I, too, have a faithful heart and am a man of my word. You may need a friend in Caesar's camp — but remember," he said with a tenderness in his voice, "whatever comes, I dedicate my life to your service. It may not be long before you will have an opportunity to put my words to the test. I'll say no more but you may be glad to know Caesar's soldier is a man of his word."

"I will remember, Senator Pudens, and from my heart I say thank you. But if you should follow me, remember, I promise nothing."

"You're leaving, gracious lady, but I follow and will guard you unseen, and hope to talk about deeper subjects than war."

He stood before her in the splendor of his manhood, holding his helmet. The sun glinted on the silvery fittings of his uniform. She rose and stood beside him, his equal in height — a dream of beauty in her simple gown. The man who had no right even to talk with her ventured, "Will it be possible to meet again?"

She quivered with this new and startling discovery, and all it would mean to her heart. And what was she to say? He looked, but no answer crossed her lips, and, with eyes deepening with a light he hadn't yet seen, she said, "I am a Christian. Your people are putting Christians to death."

"Some of my people, Princess, but not all. I beg you not to judge my nation by the few who are enamored of our imperial and cruel rulers, whose practices are openly hated. For myself, I would that the decision as to whether we shall meet again rests with you. If you would rather not see me, I will never, if possible, cross your path unless danger threatens you or yours. But I can watch over you and shall. For I know my own countrymen."

Her hand that held the flowers quivered. She replied, gazing into the far distance, "It is as God wills." And he saw a wistful sadness overshadow her face.

Soon the kindly dame waved goodbye to them, after loading them with refreshments. She beheld the young senator intently watching the cavalcade journeying west. She touched his arm, pointing to their retreating visitors. "She is above you, young man."

He turned and caught her toil-worn hand, and with an

earnestness she was surprised to see, he said, "Can you wonder, good woman, that I watch her go? It is as if the sun stopped shining. I know there is bitter and deadly strife between your nation and ours, and we are in the wrong. But, although I am not a prince, I am of noble birth, and a wealthy and large land owner."

"Does it matter, mother of British sons, into what nation we are born, so long as we do our best? Surely love breaks down every barrier and leaps over all obstacles, for I believe if it's real, it outlives death. This much I learned from my parents. I have not sought love. It exists now, to be nourished, or starved, as yonder fair maiden wills. My fate is in her keeping. Never before has any woman stirred me as your princess does, who has now passed from view."

"You're putting on airs! She is too young for marriage, I think," she said with a merry twinkle in her eyes. "You would leap before you have learned to walk. Nevertheless, Senator, my inn is open to you, and I will speak more with you later regarding the sweetest person I know."

CHAPTER IX

USK CASTLE

King Caradoc was enjoying a brief rest at Usk Castle, which could hardly be called his home, when the Avalon travellers arrived. Amidst the barking of the hounds, the entire castle accorded them a hearty welcome.

A few days later, the king sat alone in the flickering firelight, when Gladys joined him, took his great strong hand in hers and laid her head on his knee. He toyed with her shining curls, which he wound round his finger. A brief hour of reunion, overshadowed by something we call presentment. How does it come?

"Well, little one, why so silent?"

She spoke. Her musical tones always stirred him agreeably.

"My heart is full of memories tonight. I would gladly share with you."

He looked at her, wondering, for she gazed earnestly into his face.

"At Avalon I dared to take a new path, hitherto not trod by my forebears. I would impart this to you, and it may be you will turn me away. It burdens my heart, and before Rome divides our lives, I must confess my deed. Someone has won my deepest affections."

He felt her tremble. Silence fell, the hall vibrated with that mysterious something no words can describe. The king swiftly thought of their rich marriageable neighbors, wondering which he would prefer, and who would be brave enough to seek her as a wife. Gladys was his choicest and dearest possession, and the thought of losing her gave him a pang. He would be the last to let the rest of his children know this.

Feeling as if his heart had been pinched, he asked, "Who, my daughter?"

"Christ Jesus, the God of the Israel people."

The king had a momentary shock. Her glorious eyes, deep and searching, awaited his reply. Unknown to her, he had conversed with her grandfather about the Avalon missionaries. They both hoped she would outlive the attraction. Here they were wrong. Gladys could not forget or undo the seal of faith. They imagined it was just a form, little realizing it was an everlasting and unbreakable covenant.

"How can you love someone whom you do not see, who is not here, and who is dead or died?"

"He lives, Father, that's the marvel. He burst open a rock tomb. He vanished into the air like a cloud that hurries before a wind, and they saw Him no more. It was not a dead man who sailed away, but a live one. I believe as they do: *He is God.* It is such a wonderful story. Surely you are not angry."

"No child, only taken aback. Anger recoils on him who gives it birth, besides, causing hurt to one who deserves it not. I cannot live your life for you. You are still the same, only sweeter." He felt her fingers cling closer round his. "I do not hold with unduly making anyone's life unhappy for a mere selfish wish, even if it be my own kith and kin. There is little, I think, in Druidism that is to be despised. Whatever happens, speak and act the truth, whatever it costs."

"Noble father, I trust I shall never shame you because I have knelt at God's feet. I have one request. Wilt thou consent to Joseph the merchant and his friends becoming our guests here? They may, perhaps, pass near by and the winter winds are chilly." She rose and threw her arms around him, and nestled into his curly, soft beard.

"You think to win favors thus by making my heart soft as melted butter. Be it so, as you will."

Autumn's hand was tinting Nature with brown and yellow, and hawthorn berries were donning their crimson armor. Many tired plants were preparing to sleep in the bosom of the great Earth Mother, when Lleyn and Gladys, carrying fishing rods, sauntered along a valley.

Gladys loved the open hills and scudding showers as much as Lleyn, but this day she was burdened with what she wanted to tell him.

"Lleyn, Father has consented to allow the Eastern missionary and his company to rest awhile at the castle, and naturally it is a joy to me."

"Are they?" said Lleyn shortly.

Gladys couldn't understand his attitude about this subject, but bore this trial very quietly, for she had been very hurt before.

Saying he wished to push on much farther upstream, he nodded a farewell and, calling Leon, left her. He was deeply impressed by what she had told him, but concealed it. It made him restless at night, and came between him and his daily occupation. He failed to see the sudden rush of tears that blinded her.

The wintry blasts, no respecters of persons, howled dismally up the circular staircase of the castle turret and down the long passages, as the Eastern travellers sought admission at the great entrance.

The king was preparing to leave, but advanced to meet them, curious to behold these men of mystery. He was a man of few words and doer of great deeds. He noted at a glance, with an eye trained in a hard school, the faces of those whose lives had brought them in touch with God the Man. All his fear was dispelled, as with the courtly yet brisk manner of his race he bade them welcome. Men-at-arms gathered in the courtyard and his charger was led in as he said farewell.

It was short and impressive as St. Joseph raised his hand, saying, "God Almighty, bless you and yours, O King, your hearth and substance, and the kingdom you love, even unto death!"

The king rode forth deep in thought.

CHAPTER X

PRINCESS EURGAIN

Figures completely engrossed in each other lingered in the moonlight by a merry little stream that threaded its way through the meadowland near Castle Usk.

"I must leave you, beloved Eurgain, duty calls." It was Lord Salog who spoke with his deep, rich voice.

"Not so soon, we have scarcely met — and now —."

Their slow steps, crushing the sweet wild thyme, scared the little frogs. Salog stopped, taking her soft cheeks between his hands, and looking long and tenderly into her eyes, gently drew her to his heart.

Eurgain started, with a sudden remembrance of what was probably affecting their lives.

"Salog, Father left at dawn; but whatever happens, he has consented to our marriage."

"It's this new move I want to talk about, Eurgain, and it is this event which may separate us. It is essential that each of us know the other's wishes before I leave you tonight, since our separation may be lengthy, and with no means of communication. I have been ordered to stand by for a quick move north to Uriconium, where our army is concentrating." Eurgain trembled, and he held her closer. "Perhaps we are unable to talk; I have this to propose. First, marriage would simplify things for you, and I shall have the right to arrange for your future safety. For over your family creep the deep and dark shadows for which this war is responsible. You know, my dear, that Julia, my sister, loves you. She will arrange for our union at any moment, and you would be safer with her than with Caesar's soldiers."

"Oh, Salog! Poor Gladys and the others, is this to be their fate? Is there no way to prevent such a fearsome future?" Her tears fell fast; she clutched his hands and looked despairingly into his face.

"I am not in authority, Eurgain, or I would do my best. Neither of us can avert the future. What concerns us is our marriage; then you will be free of war conditions."

Eurgain drew back, hesitating. "I would feel cowardly, Salog!"

The stream rippled musically over the pebbles; the frogs croaked. Blue unearthly light fell on the girl he loved as she gazed at him perplexed.

"If you consent, Eurgain, watch daily. I will shoot an arrow into the great oak tree near the tower. Then if you are willing, and you love me enough to marry me at once, ride Pegasus as usual that morning, and join me here. Bring only what you need; we can gather up the rest when the castle is empty." She shivered.

"Oh, Salog, I am at the cross roads and I ..."

He gently took her hand, and sinking on one knee, he raised it to his lips.

"I shall have to summon Cupid to help me pull you along my road."

"Oh, Salog, but Cupid is so tiny!" Her dimpled, adorable little pits in her soft cheek made her still more attractive.

"Ha! Cupid wins, my fair one, be he ever so small. But seriously consider, and choose between two evils."

Pulling a lock of his hair gently, she said, "Rise, Salog, it is so dewy!"

Before she knew it, his strong arms imprisoned her and he kissed her fears away. She clung to him, submerged in conflicting emotions. Because of all her loved ones in grave danger — and this great and attractive escape — she felt like a bird poised for flight, yet tied.

The chilly mist rose, and their clothing became soft and limp, her hair decorated with little beads of moisture.

"Time flies, Eurgain. What is your answer?"

"Her eyes grew deep as pools, and stretching out her hands, she said, "Lead me forth; at least you are no enemy to my people."

"Your people will be mine now." A light flashed in the woods.

"Take me back, Salog — see — flickering torchlights! They

fill my heart ... with fear ... we had better skirt the wood. See, cover your armor this way." And they hurried along in silence, until she clutched his arm.

"Salog, someone is near us ... I feel as if eyes were watching. It's your soldiers ... not our folk!"

They reached the castle and she entered. He left with a great happiness, enfolded in a great anxiety.

They had been watched; soldiers were spying out the activities of the ill-fated family, for sheltering behind brambles were Caesar's men.

"Look, Marco, at our noble Salog! See what this war leads to. Bah! Cambrian maidens are like ice. I prefer the fiery beauties of Italia. I hear there is a secluded place higher up; let's find it." And in a few minutes they entered a natural little quarry, decorated with ivy and bright with crimsoning berries. Autumn was claiming its share of beauty in the reds and golds of many a leaf. It was an ideal spot for observation.

"See, Antonio, the very place," said Marco. "It commands a view of the River Usk, and the road in the meadows. No coracle (a small round boat of wickerwork covered with a waterproof layer of animal skin, canvas, etc.) can cross over unnoticed, and woe to any horseman sneaking back to the castle. He will not escape my eagle eye!"

"If your eye is awake, Marco" muttered Antonio.

"Awake! Oh, it's you, Antonio, who is the sleepyhead."Then with a gleam of merriment he clutched his companion's arm, whispering fiercely, "I have orders to post you to the north. It is your duty to report who leaves and who enters the castle."

Antonio shivered and said, "Who enters! As if I did not envy the king's huntsman Brennan that splendid buck he shot. Oh, for a hit! Alas, we have to feast on the smoke from the kitchen. I wish General Ostorius would arrive and give us something challenging to do. I hate loafing around these woods. It's all right when there are two of us. But sometimes I imagine! — and it's a bit uncanny. However, I hope we will soon be burning some of this wood to roast the king's game; don't you? And filling our bellies with mead liquor." He smacked his lips. "And the cream that floats on the milk is thick, but never have I tasted it! How wonderful to sleep under skin coverlets."

Marco looked scornfully at the speaker. "Antonio, Bacchus is no friend of yours! Castles don't fall into our mouths like apples in the orchards. Soon, my good man, you will disgrace Caesar's army. I am weary of covering up for you. Work, Antonio! Rest is sweetest when well earned." With a shy smile he rested his chin on Antonio's shoulder, and clutching his arm to prevent him from moving, whispered, "Go away! What will you do, you fearsome fellow, if perhaps you behold dead Silurians floating by like clouds — on the way to 'byd bychan' and back to Abred, and rising again?"

How alarming the weird shadows will be in the moonlight, when the wind moans like a sufferer in agony. Oh, there's a reason why you were given this post of honor and responsibility; and I think fear will keep you from slumbering on a mossy pillow."

"Marco, you heartless tormentor, I'm leaving!" And he hurried away to face the thrills of a lonely night watch.

Left alone, Marco chuckled gleefully as he looked around for a resting place against a fallen tree. He loosened his belt, removed his helmet and was soon yawning.

"I think that one night of sleep will not make much difference to Caesar after seven years!" He was just dropping off to sleep when he heard the clanking of armor which roused him. He sprang up in terror, seized his sword, crouched back against the rock behind him, his hair on end — a picture of fear. He peered through a split in the boulder which overlooked the path. He saw a face and glaring eyes like those of a cat. His blood froze as he heard a scraping noise and deep breath. "A helmet all alone!"

A tall man entered, looking around cautiously, sword in hand, ready to attack. Marco held his breath as the light fell on the naked blade of the sword. At last he saw who it was.

"Thanks to the gods, General Scapula; I feared you were an enemy!"

Ostorius Scapula was enraged. "Equip yourself. Is this Roman courage, to cringe in fear? Bah! and an armed soldier!"

Marco hastily fitted on his helmet and stood at attention, looking very sheepish. We all do when we have been discovered to be performing poorly while on duty.

"Where is the Silurian king? You are on duty here?"

"He left at daybreak, before I arrived, from what others told me. He had a large company of men with him, and they have gone north. I saw the hoof marks over there in those woods."

"Good. There will be less men to deal with." Fixing his keen eyes on Marco, he said, "Can I trust you? I need an intelligent and resourceful soldier, a silent mouth and willing obedience. If you carry out this plan, your name will be blazoned forth in the Queen of Cities, advancement will be sure, and your gift, a bulging purse."

Marco unsheathed his sword. "I swear by this; let its point pierce my heart if I divulge anything you tell me."

Good! The Britons are flagging and dissatisfied. I have here a very important document, a letter from Queen Aregwedd at Caer-Evroe (York), to King Caradoc. It is an invitation to a neighbor in difficulties. If we are able to make things unbearable for him, we hope he will accept its terms."

Marco was spellbound; his eyes grew big with this secret mission. Suddenly he said, "General, I know a British farmer called Govannan. I have often dealt with him, for he is not particular as to which side he works for. It largely depends which army pays him best and highest prices for his eggs. Shall I enlist his help, and reward him?"

"As you will, Marco. Can you not persuade that noble fellow to act for a powerful and beautiful queen? Inspire him with the honor of this secret mission. See to it, Marco, *my name* is not to be so much as muttered in his ear! Ha! ha! ha! ha! Give him something to spur him on; let it be a good bait, and promise more reward when the king is in our hands.

"He must on no account suspect me. Should he prove a failure, you had best carry this out yourself"; and he turned aside his merriment in a sneeze. "Govannan should be able to enter the Silurian camp unsuspected. Surely he must know some of the men in the army, and could be admitted on pretense of bringing them fresh eggs — or invent some tale. He might gossip about the Roman movements, and try and obtain parley with King Caradoc, telling him of the activity and determination of Rome to subdue him, or obtain his complete surrender — versus imprisonment, or death! Let him try, if thus far he is lucky, to gain the confidence of the king. By that time our plans should be perfect. I have many troops ready. I am having soldiers posted round about here. You have already received instructions, therefore pick out a reliable man in your place and hurry on this delicate mission."

"When the king is captured, the soldiers know their job, and must seize the remaining members of this family, wherever they happen to be. None of them must be allowed to remain. Remember, no violence! I go on to Uriconium, and within a few days the king should be there, and all the other prisoners as well, pending the emperor's decision as to their destination. Soon we shall be breathing the soft airs of Italia. Here is my ring. Guard it well; it will admit you to her presence; and here is also a well-filled purse for the venture. As for Govannan, persuade him to enter the British camp, say, two or three days after his first visit. Remember, both of you, the queen is a traitoress, serpent-like, and her sting is cruel. Be equally alert and resourceful and attentive to her commands. Once the British lion is in her castle, all will be well."

Drawing his sword, he swung it round his head joyfully. "At last Rome is in sight! Away, Marco! Silence, there's not a moment to lose."

Marco saluted, and cautiously walked away, the proudest soldier in Caesar's army, while his superior rocked to and fro with suppressed merriment that the first man had swallowed the bait. To muffle his laughter he pressed his cloak over his mouth, lest Marco hearing, should become suspicious.

"Ah, Marco! From what are you not saving me? You have shouldered the responsibility, and if you fail, the blame on you will fall. Ha! Ha! Ha! Ha! But I take the credit — should success crown those plans. May the queen's dream come true; and if the gods are propitious, then indeed I may ride triumphantly through the city of Rome with 'Caradoc in Chains' walking beside me!"

CHAPTER XI

KING CARADOC'S BETRAYAL

Many fearsome days dragged on. The autumn sunshine mocked anxious hearts, waiting for dreaded news which never came. For there was an overwhelming combination. A concentrated effort to overcome King Caradoc's army was being made by Aulus Plautius, aided by Ostorius Scapula, who was laying his plans to entrap the king at "Castra Ostorii," in "Dinder, Herefordshire, now ludicrously corrupted into Oyster-Hill," ("St. Paul in Britain") and Queen Aregwedd's Brigantine army, helped by the Iceni in the north. Vespasian and Titus, his son, were more than lightly pushing westward from Verulam.

The shadows of Castle Usk were lengthening. The evening was still with the touch of frost, the woods glorious in their autumn tints, as the two young princesses and Lleyn strolled into the woods, discussing the absence of news. Eurgain stopped, pointing to a man. "Lleyn, I am sure it is Oswain. What could have happened?" They hurried forward.

Questioned, he replied as follows:

"I am not well, so King Caradoc sent me back to relate what is taking place. As far as we know, the two Roman generals are endeavoring to entangle your father, my king. We had marched well, and at last were seated round a cauldron of lovely broth, when a traitor entered the camp, a native, too, called Govannan, who appeared as a farmer, carrying a basketful of beautiful eggs. I bought some for the king, but I took a great dislike to that man. He had a glib tongue, and informed us that the day before he had made a good sale of eggs in the Roman camp some miles away. They were very kind, and gave him food, did him well; and he looked like it, too. He told us that in conversation the Romans feared the Brigantines were again beginning to be friendly to us Silurians, as if we wouldn't be the first to rejoice if this were so. Then he said that Queen Aregwedd was reviewing her army, riding a great horse, looking beautiful — but severe in her orders — and some garbled conversation about an important letter or message which was to be delivered to King Caradoc; but I wouldn't believe a word he said. I began to be suspicious and hated the man, and on my hips I planted my fists and pressed my feet firmly in the soil. "You look quite combative," he remarked.

" 'Maybe,' I replied, 'these are war days. Are you for Caradoc or Caesar, or Aregwedd, who is Caesar's cat, out to catch a British mouse for a Roman tiger! Bah! From gossip Govannan has mighty fine claws. A cat, a mouse and a tiger, are no match for a British lion! Out, cringing coward; speak the truth, you mongrel,' I roared. his eyes rolled round under their lids like pebbles in a flowing stream, and he pretended to be rearranging his basket, and avoiding my eyes said, 'For King Caradoc, indeed. I am of Celtic stock. What do you take me for, one who isn't true to my country?'

" 'Maybe,' I retorted, very irritated, 'but you do not possess a true spirit of our race, or you would have joined the king's army. We need men, you hefty, lazy lout. Away with your eggs'; and I kicked his half-empty basket out of his hand. How our men laughed. 'Anyway,' one remarked, 'these are not 'The Lays of Ancient Rome.' ' I shook my sword before his eyes. 'Lay hold of a fighting sword, you shirker, and let us prick your arm and behold with our own eyes the color of your blood, and judge whether it be Cambrian or Roman. Ah! Coward, you don't like the look of my sword nor my words.' He scowled at me, and slunk away with a nasty snarl like a fighting dog, but without a word. Bah!

"As ill luck would have it, he met your father, the king, on his way to his tent. After saluting, he spoke with him.

"Later that day when I was serving my royal master he told me that Govannan was very mysterious about some sealed document written by Queen Aregwedd, which probably had to do with terms of alliance and reconciliation between the Silurians and the Brigantes. Our king master replied, 'We seek no second-hand information. See to it that you deliver my words first-hand to all who may be interested and to all who desire to make peace on such terms. I will fight to a finish against foreign or British foe. I am willing to die, if need be for my country. Begone! Sell no more eggs in my camp.' "

By this time they approached the castle, and Oswain wearily entered.

That night Eurgain prepared to leave the castle, for it could be only a question of hours now, she calculated, before Salog's feathered messenger would be in the tree. She had decided on flight; the alternative seemed a gloomy enough prospect.

She crept into the chamber where Gladys slept and looked tenderly at the lovely sleeper as she lay on her couch, tears still wet beneath her long lashes. She bent and kissed her shining wavy hair, murmuring softly, "I wonder why we are so different. You have always loved father, and he always loved you more than me, and I have resented this; yes, and it is also true I have envied you your beauty. When shall we meet again — and where — if ever, for once Rome divides us — what then?"

She sought her own couch and coiled up to snatch a little sleep before dawn.

The sunlight was creeping down the bark of the trees as it rose above the hills when she woke. She searched for and found the arrow was really there, hastily clothed herself and sped swiftly and noiselessly over the rushes, and gently slid back the great oak beam of the castle gate. The patrolling soldier was walking towards the great round tower. There was no difficulty, as she was often up early and out, and her light fingers soon dislodged the marriage messenger, her first love letter, and opened it with flushed cheek. But her heart gripped painfully as she read its contents.

"Your father has fallen into some trap, and is to all intents a doomed man. A strong escort of our army accompanied him to Urconium, and as far as I can gather they journey to Caer Evroe, (York — to the Palace of Queen Aregwedd.) but I know too little to say more. Events are marching on, and for your family so disastrously. Think before it is too late for me to help you, my beloved one. With them you will share their fate. As my wife you will be safe and unmolested, and Julia is a real dear and is arranging for our union. You will be able to help them, I hope. I hear from various sources some document was handed to King Caradoc, and without any escort from his men, whom he seems to have sent back, he went with them.

"His devoted followers, uneasy, followed to gain word and explanation, but our men were patrolling the roads and threatened to fight them if they followed, so they returned to raise the alarm, thoroughly crestfallen; and undoubtedly, had your father refused, they would have used violence. There is an idea that Queen Aregwedd has some scheme and is going to stand by the king; but she, I know, favors Claudius, and is assured that ultimate victory will be ours. Of course, if she has veered round and intends to stand by Siluria, that will be an astonishing event. In that case it will check us, and there will be serious days ahead for our troops. But I do not believe it, for Aregwedd is a dangerous friend — and a still more dangerous enemy. She bears no love for your father. In any case, I shall await your decision by the little bridge, listening for the thudding hoofs of Pegasus in the sweet meadow thyme. There I await my bride with a beating heart, and eyes that search the woodland path for your form. Keep silent; do not leave this letter behind.
Salog.

With trembling fingers Eurgain tied a small bundle on to her saddle cloth and, wrapping a warm cloak round her, rode joyfully through the morning mist. The castle guard, to whom this was a daily occurence, saluted her, and waving to him she sped away to where her lover waited.

A short note of farewell to Gladys lay near her couch:

"I am sorry, Gladys, not to say goodbye to you, but it is better this way, I am going to meet Salog. Don't be anxious; before the day is over we shall be united. Julia is a dear. She is in our secret, and is kindly arranging all for me, and do not forget Father did give his consent.

"Salog says as his wife I shall be able to help you more. I trust so. I am not heartless, and believe me, I have been feeling it all very much.
Eurgain."

CHAPTER XII

PRINCESS GLADYS

Gladys read the brief note from her sister, and knew it was useless to follow her. It only confirmed the uneasy premonitions that things were seriously wrong, and it increased her depression.

By chance for one reason or another her brothers were out. Lleyn, hearing that Brennen, King Caradoc's herdsman, was troubled by a bear doing much damage to the flock, had gone to assist him.

Hour after hour passed, and no tidings reached her from the outside world. It was not safe to venture far; but, unable to remain in the castle longer, she threw a warm cloak over her shoulders and set forth for the higher woods, accompanied by their great hound Leon, full of delight, a contrast to his heavy-hearted mistress. Her exit from the castle had been observed by eyes other than those of the home-guard.

A Roman soldier, hiding in the ivy of a large tree, at last had the opportunity he had waited for so long. He watched her retreating form, and waited until the guard, now greatly reduced, had walked in the opposite direction. He had used every available shelter and move both swiftly and silently along because of Leon, who already had sniffed round the path suspiciously.

She lingered gathering blackberries. The man who followed stalked her like any forest deer, and had some difficulty to keep her in sight without exposing himself. How little she knew of the danger that dogged her steps, or the fate that was to overwhelm her.

She entered the small quarry, and sat on a slab of rock, her elbows in her hands. Wistfully her eyes swept over the humble homesteads of her father's retainers; here and their some with their men missing, or dead, or fighting.

Mournfully she wondered what would be the result of it all, and shivered at the possibility of death to one she loved, or imprisonment; nay, it was unthinkable with so many attached to him. Surely Oswain's tales were foolish ones.

The wind stirred her curls as she rested her eyes on the castle, their temporary home, some distance from the palace at Llantwit Major. It appealed to her, surrounded by its leafy guardians, for autumn had retinted the green leaves, now rich yellow and russet brown. The sombre walls and towers covered with ivy, had no eerie terrors. She loved every stone in it. Suddenly she thought of Pudens — a wild thought, an unborn hope — that perhaps he might be able to help them. It was but a fleeting thought, which gradually became real; but pride forbade its acceptance. her lips moved. "He promised to stand by me, but how can I get a message to him, and where is he, and what could I say? It's impossible; and besides, although he seemed true, at heart he may be false!"

She felt sadder than before, and along with it the rankling bitterness against this foreign nation, causing them all such misery and heartbreak.

She vividly recalled their meeting as he stood before her in his picturesque Roman uniform and the strength and beauty of early manhood, courteous and considerate; and with polished manners so different to her brusque countrymen. She recalled the way he raised her rosebud to his lips. His earnest words: "You may need a friend in the enemy's camp" — a warning of what?

His pathetic request, a challenge — to trust him — and again that she would probably have the chance to prove his word. "He cannot surely be a real enemy. No, but there, I shall know if we meet again. Why do I keep thinking of him and hungering for a sight of his face? Alas, woe to this interest, it is doomed to perish."

Then home sorrows surged up; she began to feel the strain of watching for someone to appear, or something to happen; it was nerve racking. Absorbed in introspective reveries, she failed to see Leon's ears raised sniffing the air as he slowly rose to inspect those who approached. "Don't be suspicious, old boy. It's Lleyn, I expect returning from the hills; maybe with a buck." And she stroked his silky head. But Leon did more; ominous growls increased.

She rose, and shading her eyes, tried to discover who the body of horsemen were skirting the river. They came nearer, and she saw they were Roman soldiers; and horrors! They were turning towards the castle.

So intently was she watching the strange cavalcade she failed to hear stealthy footsteps advancing towards the quarry.

Leon suddenly turned, showing his teeth, growling fiercely and would have leaped forward had she not gripped his collar when a helmet appeared above the boulder.

She dragged Leon towards her and shrank back against the ivy, her heart thumping terribly, for she was thoroughly alarmed. The actions of these men who came and broke up homes, leaving trails of misery and sorrow behind, crossed her mind. And she was alone, although the dog would have to be reckoned with. She was white to the lips.

The man entered and paused within a few paces without speaking. At last she gained courage to look at the intruder, and met the eyes of Senator Pudens. Politely he bowed, saying, "I am extremely sorry, Princess, to intrude this way. I'm afraid I have startled you cruelly, but time is so short, and what I have to say, so urgent, this must be my excuse.

"You have, perhaps, observed that company. It is of them I would tell you. They have been sent here by order of Ostorius Scapula, and they are searching for your family. For you must be informed that your father ... is ... a prisoner of war ..."

She clutched at her throat and gazed at him horrorstruck, but he had no time to sympathize.

"I have approached the governor, Aulus Plautius, and have volunteered to act as one of the escort which are to accompany the royal prisoners."

Gladys gazed at him incredulously, terror-struck, until he wished she were at the end of the earth, or anywhere out of sight of her pain.

She was panting, and blurted out, "What do you mean, Senator Pudens? You say that my father is a prisoner of war. Why?"

"All of your family will be in due time; it is Caesar's command."

"What about my grandfather, the Arch-Druid?"

"Certainly! He and the others."

"But we do not fight! How cruel!" She staggered back against the rock.

"Listen carefully, Princess; a lot depends on what I say, and time is flying. I have closed my large villa at Chichester in order to be within reach, for I volunteered to be one of the officers in charge of your people. There is a soldier named Marco — a lazy and kind-hearted man — but under a cruel general, Ostorious Scapula. I helped Marco, and he owes me for it. In all sincerity," he added, drawing nearer her and holding her limp hand, "will you trust 'Caesar's soldier'? I will guard you as I would my mother, and will die rather than let any harm come to you; and will do my best for those whom you love."

He moved nearer, and said in his pleading voice, vibrating with emotion, "Remember we are friends." He added in a whisper, with his eyes fixed on her, "I wish we were more, but this is no time to speak of the heart quest — and, Princess, whatever we are to each other, we had better pretend we are strangers. It will be wiser that our escort think I am simply Caesar's officer, for — how can I tell you? It is better that you know that the destination of all the prisoners is Rome."

"Rome!" gasped Gladys. "How unjust!" She clutched his arm to steady herself. "Is this possible with such loyal hearts that surround my father?"

"I'm afraid so. I wish it were not. Queen Aregwedd — she is your father's relative, I've been told — has sided with us. She lured your father to her castle, and while he was there, she had him put in chains. She is a dangerous, jealous woman. I admire the king, your father and wish I were in his army instead of ..."

Tears gathered under her long lashes. Pudens felt reproachful, saying in his heart, "I would rather fight in open warfare than inflict such misery as this."

Gladys moved, and looked down at the home that was to know her no more. He heard her whisper, "Poor Father!"

Pudens was nervous, fearing every minute that he would be seen, for it would have made their fate harder. He lifted her listless hands, cold as ice, and tried to warm them. Her head was still turned away, her eyes fixed abstractly on the castle as she bade her lifetime farewell, and his voice reached her as if he were along way off.

A shout made her start and shiver.

"Do I dare say what is in my heart? And I know this is not a fitting time to say it, but — sweet woman — you have become the most precious thing in my lonely life. Since we parted at the hospice, my love and devotion have cried out to see you once again, and this is the coveted hour, laden only with pain I would gladly shield you from, and it is I who have had to do it."

His face was pinched up with distress. After a few minutes' struggle he continued, "If I knew that at some time in a happier day you would consent to be my wife, how I would try to compensate for some of this hateful business. But whatever you answer, either yes or no, I will do my best to alleviate the sufferings and trials that my country is causing you and yours to endure."

Gladys stood rigid, her face set as if frozen into a marble statue. Pudens was greatly distressed and alarmed. "Forgive me, I beg you," he whispered.

She licked her dry lips, her throat parched from the shock of one blow after another and swaying perilously.

"What can I do? Oh, don't answer, Princess. I am cruel to say all this just now, but I hoped — and I fear without any chance for a response from you! I am greatly punished." He wiped the moisture from his brows which this agonizing interview had cast over them. He realized the time was passing and that a cruel fate was approaching her with stealthy strides.

"If you have doubts as to my sincerity of these promises, Princess, I will swear by the gods that ..."

And with a sudden movement she recovered from her mental paralysis and sprang toward him; the blood rushed into her ashen cheeks. Then she laid her finger on his lips, momentarily causing him to step back.

"I am a Christian maid. What are Pagan gods to me? Statues carved out of Carrara marble. I have heard they are beautiful, breathless, utterly lifeless!"

Her lovely eyes were ringed with the shadow of her anguish, gazing at him searchingly, as if trying to ascertain the deep things that were confronting her.

"If you love me, Pudens, I ask you to record it before my God, a Living Being from whom all love proceeds. He fills that universe, invisible in the heavens," she said, looking up, raising her hand to the sky as if appealing to Him she knew dwelt there in space.

The light wind rustled the crisp leaves round their feet as they stood, their hearts on a rack.

Senator Pudens forgot all except the girl he had learned to love, marvelling at the tremendous power of her splendid character. It was the birth-pangs of deep devotion, which caused her heart to throb violently — the intensely human desire versus the higher call to self-sacrifice.

In an absent voice, as if speaking to herself, she said: "I am sealed as God's child. Listen" — and she turned and looked at Pudens — "He seeks you, Pudens, who asks me to share your life. Here we two stand before God — with this great thing that has to be answered ... some day. For myself, what can I say? I am bewildered." She raised her glistening eyes and met his deepening with the intensity of his love which drew hers forth.

As a butterfly emerges from its chrysalis and painfully its beautiful crumpled wings are spread out from its narrow cradle, and trembling, are filled with life and power for flight, so her love cast off its uncertainty and pain.

Pudens waited until the splendid girl, so unlike the soft, luxurious womanhood of the south, turned voluntarily to him. How he yearned for her; but he was wise enough to give her time, and only longed to do the best for her. Would she yield? She faced more than he knew. He stood as folks stand in all ages, but Gladys had drunk deeply, and had recently taken a tremendous step, and obeyed a spiritual call. Young as she was, she knew it might cause estrangement and many difficulties. That she loved him now, and loved him for always, she knew it only too well.

Gladys knew the difference in their ideals, and their national difference. Would love be strong enough to hold? Ah! every part of her rushed forward towards this man who had stormed the citadel of her heart, and yet she could, she knew, resist. But some fate — the future maybe, and God working to call her to her destiny and high position — prevailed.

Thus these minutes seemed an eternity.

She read in his eyes the fidelity of a faithful heart, and with an appealing little movement, her eyes suffused with tears, she held out her hands, claiming the comfort he longed to give her.

It was a mute appeal that touched him deeper than words; and who can wonder that his arms stole around her trembling form. Thus they stood, speech had taken to itself wings.

His senses, keyed up as to their peril, started as a tiny twig broke. With a hurried glance he breathed, "Till death, my Gladys. I say this with solemn intention before the One you call God. To you I will be faithful."

A robin puffed out his crimson breast, chanting his chippy and homely ditty; the wind rustled through the trees,, scattering golden leaves around them.

"Till death, Pudens, and then beyond in Paradise."

"I know nothing of such a place — but with you ... ah!"

"God willing, Pudens, as your wife, in your house, in Italy, if God wills it, I will teach you."

They heard the voices of the search party scouring the woods, looking for the young princess and any of the others.

With one long embrace Pudens leaped up the rocks and hid in the overhanging trees, witnessing the most sickening sight of his life — the capture of the royal maiden, his affianced wife, for no fault. He was powerless to avert the cruel order of Caesar.

Gladys quietly submitted and walked down between the soldiers in a dream, leading Leon, who growled ominously, without one glance to betray her lover to their officer.

The amazed family, and a few attendants, gathered together needful belongings.

They mounted Gladys on one of her father's beautiful horses, for which he was famous, allowing her to keep Leon.

She moved mechanically, as a sleep-walker. Everything seemed swaying round her in a terrible tangle, beyond her power to unravel. Was it real or a bad dream, she wondered, too stunned to think. In fact, they feared she would fall; she swayed dizzily, holding on, fearing she would faint.

Thus they journeyed through England's fair garden, and were joined by one group after another of her woe-stricken family.

A cavalcade clattered up to to an appointed meeting place, and her heart sank as she beheld her grandfather Bran with her great grandfather Llyr Lladiath, and her three brothers, Cellyn, Cynon and Lleyn.

To attempt to converse or protest was useless. Their silence showed the agony each one endured.

The unwarranted cruelty of this Roman deed speaks volumes. Their circumstances seemed to freeze all feelings. It was a merciless action to involve all those indirectly irresponsible persons.

Eventually they reached Uriconium (Wrekin). There fresh heartbreaks awaited them as they beheld King Caradoc riding his own splendid horse, surrounded by a bodyguard, his great charger led. He sat speechless, in proud unconquered dignity, with stern face, his blue eyes flashing dangerously, as he encountered the wistful ones of those he loved in a like fate. But never a word was uttered. So the British monarch and his family were betrayed by British blood.

Elated were the traitoress, Queen Cortismandua and her Roman accomplice, for their plans were completed beyond their expectations.

There were three royal families that were conducted to prison, from the great, great grandfather to the great grandchildren, without permitting one of them to escape.

First the family of Llyr Llediaith, who were carried to prison at Rome by Cesaridae ... not one or another of them escaped. They were the most complete incarcerations of families known.

As we look back across the centuries we ask, maybe, Was it worth while?

Assuredly!

It is only as we look back at some unspeakable suffering that we know the light was veiled; so that events beyond our comprehension might come to fruition. Lives are linked to a great chain, and link by link the Maker tests its strength.

So that chain lives, and we are joined to its antiquity, and are the better for their sufferings.

THE FIRST FORUM

PART II

CHAPTER I

PALATIUM BRITANNICUM

A handsome youth rode leisurely along the wooded banks of the Tiber one gorgeous morning; a cantata of song, as the feathered denizens of the woods serenaded their mates, building homes for their young. On the naked branches, soft green leaves peeped out of their tight jackets. In the long grass, heavy with dew, chirped the grilli. (small beetles, gathered for luck and caged)

The young senator was lost in thought, resplendent in gala attire, his toga folded to a nicety, evidently bound for some fiesta. His spendid steed tossed his head and curveted in his best style, for he had had extra attention paid to his silky coat. Behind the young nobleman rode Luigi, his attendant, also well mounted, carrying a magnificent bouquet.

On the river were small fishing boats, from which snatches of song floated over the water. Along the banks great fishing nets were suspended, swaying to and fro in the breeze, ready for use.

Riding over one of the bridges were a few jovial and noisy youths; one wag had hung flowers round the neck of his horse. Seeing the young senator, they shouted, "Greetings Pudens, on this, your wedding day."

Friends are a very happy possession, but today, the young senator wished them farther, and he was disinclined to be courteous to the good-natured guests who had inadvertantly crossed his path.

Antonio, spying a flower in his belt, said: "So you bear a white rose befitting this great occasion. It is not often a princess is the bride. May she lay no heavier burden on you than that exquisite bloom. Well, I approve, so all is well. I think you have chosen wisely for one so wealthy, for she will not encourage you to squander your fortune in magnificent banquets."

Amedeo, another friend, rode up mysteriously, and leaning towards him, said: "It is for us to console the broken-hearted belles! For myself, I still delight in banquets where the beauty of Rome has no rival; our emperors see to that. The purple grapes still grow; although the gallant gentleman who rides beside me upholds the qualities of the mead flagon of the British. But there, Pudens, you have long forsaken us. What do you say, Antonio, to this speech? And I am only half awake. Early to bed and early to rise is not to be encouraged!"

Yes, my friend!" replied Antonio; "our senator is somewhat changed since his duties took him to the Emerald Isle of the British. I think the charms of Sanimum with a lovely wife will separate us still more, for East will wed with West, the combination — what? Success or failure? — Who knows? Ah well, we will serenade the lover, and wave him off with the rose of Britain."

"True Amedeo," said Pudens, "I plucked a bloom that grew in a Cambrian garden. What are the faded flowers of Rome to me! Some day perhaps you, too, will find one. Who then having found one would be satisfied with the passing excitement of depthless emotions. For it is unwise to call passion love; for passion is not love; anymore than the perfume is the plant from which it flows. You are still unwed; choose well, and carefully, or you will be sorry."

Antonio, with mocking merriment, shot a swift glance at the gallant youth riding to his fiesta, and said to the others, "Did you hear these wise words of advice?"

Pudens, in no mood to talk, rode on ahead.

"We did, Antonio, but he is to be excused ... for ... well ... there! He knows we are happy and steeped in the glamour of this city of romance and license. To put restraint on as a bridle on a horse, ah! It's unthinkable.

"Christians have some wondrous tale about life after death; about that I know nothing. Today is mine, I am alive and intend to drink the joys of life as I desire them, and take part of the festival of the gods instead of treading the dust of the amphitheatre for some future bliss."

They rounded the last corner, and before them stood the stately palace which was even then becoming famous.

The Palatium Britannicum was the home of the Welsh king.

His enforced exile still had to run five more years before Rome set him free. It seems the exception that he had escaped with his life, as the reverse was meted out to captured foes. We may be sure it was with no ungrateful heart that he was able to live in such a noble mansion; numerically the staff of servers must have been very large.

Perhaps Rome was wise enough to realize that victory, complete victory, was still an elusive ideal not yet within their grasp. Celebrated Roman officials, such as Vespasian and Titus and others, were still fighting the Islanders, and any harm befalling such a beloved ruler as the Silurian monarch would undoubtedly have had serious consequences, raising still more animosity against many whose homes had sprung up in a land that was not and could not be theirs.

The nuptial day of Senator Pudens and the Welsh princess dawned full of promise over the Italian hills.

The palace was colorfully decorated; loving hands were putting the last touches to the flowers; all were happy and delighted. It was both a home and a sanctuary, for seemingly already Pastor Hermas conducted services there. (Until the reign of Constantine the Roman Christians had no other church than the Titulus to worship in. — St. Paul in Britain)

The sleeping chamber of the young princess opened out on to a wide balcony. She stood alone, leaning against the parapet, dreamily gazing out over the hazy scene. She had dismissed her attendants, who left her attired in her long silk tunic, a golden belt fastened by a Celtic clasp confined it to her waist — a gift from home friends.

Below, the murmer of many voices as the guests entered and walked in the peristyle and colonaded courts. For this was a very popular wedding, and, of course, quite extraordinary.

Tears glistened under her long lashes, for, in truth, not only was she marrying a man of a foreign nation, but she was leaving her father in peculiarly trying circumstances. The Romans were still causing untold misery to her own people as well as the rest of her native land. It was not a question of love, for that had been severely tested. But the sudden hesitation that enveloped her was that Pudens was not a Christian, and in those days, perhaps, it meant greater barriers between husband and wife. She had proof of this — even then. No, she was too loyal to break so sacred a promise as they had exchanged in the quarry, the day of her arrest; nor did she want to. Her marriage opened up possibilities of influencing a great number of persons, as a lady of culture and wealth. Nevertheless, it had been her secret hope that he would have been converted before their union. She had watched for dawn to break over ignorance and idolatry, as a mother watches her waking infant. But in sorrow she had learned she could no more raise to life a dead and unconverted heart than a plant would mature because a long-delayed sunbeam had kissed its roots. It needed the miraculous touch of the Great Spirit to work this miracle.

But he had, to her joy, consented that any children born to them should follow her faith. It was barely twenty years since the Crucifixion, and Christianity was slowly and painfully breaking up idolatrous practices.

Where should we be today, had the living witnesses, men and women like ourselves, and far more ignorant, withheld their testimony to the miraculous doings in Palestine!

They faithfully proclaimed the Deity of the Son of Man, as God Incarnate, and that beyond the grave was life eternal for believers of Jesus Christ. They risked their lives in announcing this. What might have happened had they remained silent about the Messiah, as the world's future King, heir of the Davidic line, or failed to demonstrate the irrestible attraction of a Living God versus gods of marble or stone, is beyond imagination's borderland and unanswerable.

Superhuman qualities mark those brave hearts crowned with martyr's seals. Those "babes in Christ" faced hungry infuriated animals and worse. Do we shrink from home trials? They had theirs! Are we too spoon-fed, too soft, to face any opposition? Do we, happy in luxurious religious freedom, bitterly criticize those who try to minister to our souls? We owe our inherited faith to those appalling and blood-curdling scenes in the Coliseums in Italy, France, Spain and elsewhere.

But let us return to our young friend living in that age, which brought out the purest human qualities.

She lingered alone, except for Leon, her great hound, whose faithful eyes watched her as he lay crouching nearby — the king's gift, to accompany her to her new home. The light wind stirred her draperies and sported with the little ringlets that framed her face, like waves breaking over her high and intellectual forehead. Behind, her beautiful hair rippled over her glistening robe, ending in adorable curls, the plaything of all who loved her best.

She became suddenly overwhelmed. It was a great turning-point, a crisis, and we all know that it surges up unsought and almost leaves one breathless. She cried out aloud:

"It is not too late, O Lord. What is your will for us?

The silence was broken by the cooing of doves, a mystic message from the heavens reached her. Let those who can explain these things. They come, dispersing every shadow, with an unmistakable "All is well." With a quick sigh of relief she flung her arms around Leon, tucked Pudens' lovely rosebud into her girdle, and picked up the three ears of corn which Roman brides were accustomed to carry, symbolic of plenty, and maybe the forerunner of wedding cakes.

She descended the broad stairway to the courtyard, now ablaze with sunshine, where garlands swung between the pillars and great ropes of flowers wound round them.

Her appearance caused no little stir, for she was late. She walked with great dignity, responding to many smiles. But it was the king she sought, whose eyes devoured her with wistful tenderness. Of all his children he did love her best, and this dreadful separation was all the harder to bear because of his circumstances.

They stood aloof amidst all their guests, lost in that deep sympathy and devotion with only such hearts as they had could hold. Words were dangerously near to tears to be uttered.

The palace, as to decorations, was a curious mixture of Western and Mediterranean magnificence. Rare skins from Cambrian hills were spread on the beautiful Roman pavement. Even the walls were adorned with antlers of the red deer and other elegant creatures. There, too, the beautiful shield that had protected the heart of a British hero, plus his bridle and sword. His bow, too, with its twelve arrows, reviving sad memories of prowess for a captive king's eyes to rest on.

He had altered nothing of his attire, and wore his torque collar. That day he had donned a new mantle held in position by a massive Celtic clasp — enamel and gold.

But these sweet stolen minutes fled, and others claimed their attention.

The king knew how proud Gladys was and how hard was this enforced stay in Italy. Pudens, unfailingly devoted, had eased them as much as he dared, having spared neither money nor influence with the Roman officials on their behalf.

Outside the portico the bridegroom, attended by his jovial friends ready for everything which was form of entertainment, slowly dismounted. For today he loitered, whereas before he had bounded up the marble steps. Antonio, winking at Amedeo, gently pushed him forward. The air was fragrant with heavy flowers as they walked up between waving palms.

"Pudens is nervous," whispered Antonio in his ear, and digging him in the ribs he said aloud: "Surely, Pudens, you will not turn back when such a rare prize awaits you, or surely I'll be the first to console the sad-hearted maiden from 'The Isles of the West.' "

With heightened color, Pudens took the bouquet Luigi held and nervously advanced towards the royal group. He was cordially received, and introduced his friends. His eager eyes searched for the girl he loved, for, do what he would, he felt awed. He realized it was no ordinary union.

He might have been wedding a goddess, for he held her in high esteem. That he loved her devotedly there was no shadow of doubt. But — there was just that something — that was distant which came in between them, and that was her faith.

He met her glance and her radiant smile, and then he knelt and presented his bouquet. She took it, and he bent and kissed her forehead. And drawing from his pouch his gift, he laid a chain of beautiful pearls over her head.

Thus it came about that Pudens, mentioned in St. Paul's

Epistle, (II Tim. iv., 21.) bore away his Celtic bride, Gladys — now Claudia of the New Testament — to his country estate.

Years later it was the exiled king's greatest joy when Princess Claudia brought her lusty boy Timotheus, and a serious-eyed little girl whom they named Pudentiana, on a visit to their grandfather at Palatium Britannicum. When the king was allowed to visit their home, before he left, or soon after, another child was born whom they named Novatus, and finally a daughter Praxedes.

One great event crowned the young wife's happiness. it was Pudens' conversion.

In spite of her growing family, at the age of twenty-four, Gladys had become celebrated on account of her poems and hymns.

Princess Gladys is lost to us now, and henceforth becomes the Roman matron, renamed *Claudia* (2 Tim., iv, 21). She is sometimes called "Claudia Britannica," renamed out of compliment to the Emperor Claudius, who was greatly interested in her.

King Caradoc, Caractacus of school fame, returned to Britain at the end of his seven years' retention. During his absence King Arviragus had been elected to fill his place as Pendragon, and to all intents and purposes carried on splendidly.

"Has our great enemy, Arviragus, the divan chair-borne British king, dropped from his battle-throne?" Thus wrote Juvenal. Had such been the case, Romans would have felt "intense satisfaction."

According to The Rev. Morgan's account, General Ostorius Scapula was weary of this opposition, and requested to be freed from military duties in Britain.

At last the day dawned when the Pudentius family bade farewell to King Caradoc.

He gave them his palace on Mons Sacre, the Hospitium Britannicum, or Hospitium Apostolorum, finally called "The Titulus."

Today in Rome it is called "Chiesa di S. Pudenziana." (the Church of St. Pudenziana).

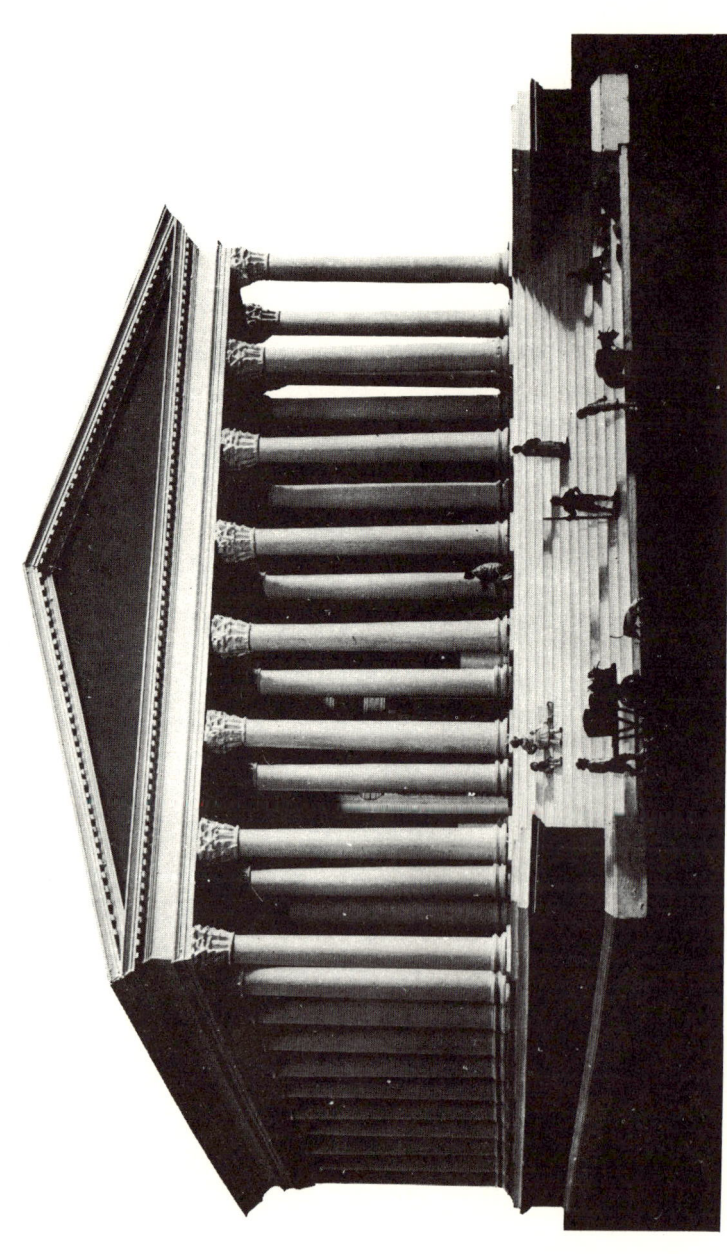

Model of the temple of Claudius at Camulodunum, founded about AD 50. It was the largest Roman temple in Britain, the main building being about 39 × 30 yards (35 × 27 m). Sandstone, alabaster, plaster mouldings and many foreign marbles were used in its construction. Colchester Keep, the largest in Britain, uses the base of the temple for foundations.

PART II
CHAPTER II

CASTELLO SAMNIUM

Prince Lleyn, renamed Linus, was resident in Italy along with the rest of his family. Once so agile and fleet of foot, a lover of heather-clad hills, he now, faithful to duty's call, trudged wearily beside his languid horse, up and up beneath the intense heat of an Italian sun.

As bishop, he had been singled out by St. Paul to carry the infant Church through some of its most perilous days. For Claudius Caesar had as his successor Nero, of world fame for cruelty; followed by other imperial rulers, all deadly enemies to the faith.

He pressed forward to visit his sister, Princess Claudia, intending to accompany Paul, their august visitor, back to Rome.

He paused beneath an olive tree and wiped the sweat from his brow, but the tree afforded little protection. He searched the hills, through the hazy heat, with his tired eyes and smiled as he beheld the goal of his pilgrimage.

This castle was constructed to be a secure refuge in case of unfriendly neighbors, when vendettas, outlawry, and brigandage were usual occurrences.

The castle itself was square built, tucked into a fold of the hills. There was only one long, winding road, none too good, on account of water-courses that had carved out miniature river beds for themselves. The road wound up through olive groves, the poderies, adorned by clusters of grapes.

"When the evening shadows lengthen and the busy world is hushed," the mystic notes, elusive, thrilling in their purity, roll out from the slim body of the nightingales perched on some branch; silhouetted against a clear primrose sky.

Beneath the trees millions of sportive fireflies tremble their fairy lamps in sheer joy of life, so the saying is, flickering to scare away the mice from the crops. Then the aquatic orchestra tunes up. The deep-throated croaking of the toads. Each sings its own note, seated on a leafy throne in a stagnant pond.

Such is an Italian summer, nightly. Until sleep, cheated of its repose by mosquitoes singing a lullaby near your ear, the chorus outside, you feel inclined to throttle all, as the toads eventually throttle their parents!

Sheltering beneath the sombre walls were the homes of the farmers, living alongside their padrone's castle. Perchance the click-clack of the heavy hand-looms worked by the native women will be heard. Their skilled hands make the shuttles fly merrily as they sing to their livestock beside them.

Above, on the kitchen rafters, chestnuts are drying, stored for the lean days when the wheat flour is used up — for it grows poorly amidst the stones.

It is cut and laid on dry cow-dung, thrashed out by men swinging hand flails, as they stand opposite to one another, the breeze carrying away the chaff.

Chestnuts then become the staple food. They are crushed, mixed with water, baked between hot stones; eaten as pink, sweet and indigestible cakes.

On the ground floor are estate offices under arches which support a wide terrace above. There is the lemon house; the lemons grow in pots and are carried out in summer and brought inside when the winter winds begin.

From the fortified west tower is a sloping path, carved out of living rock. Easy steps terminate on a broad terrace which encircles the castle on three sides, and is the ground floor of the owners. From this level it is the delight of the inhabitants to follow the winding goat tracks in and out the bend of the hills, which lead up to breezy heights, or down to the breathless valleys and adjacent baths. These baths were known subsequently as Thermae Timothinae and Thermae Novatinae. The palace baths and grounds were bequeathed by Timotheus to the Church at Rome. And these were the only buildings of any magnitude possessed by the Roman Church till the reign of Constantine."
— St. Paul in Britain (Morgan).

Here could be seen and heard the shepherdess and her flocks.

A visitor had to follow the rock path up on to the terrace, which bent round outside the castle, and would find themselves on the south side, where oleanders, together with feathery palms and mimosa waved over divans and handsome oriental rugs. To enter the living part of the castle, it was necessary to pass through heavy gates, now thrown back against the walls of a high archway that divided the building into two halves.

On one side grew a wisteria and magnolia. Opposite, clinging to the hoary walls, an ancient vine, now laden with luscious grapes, whose leaves were mottled with autumn's gorgeous coloring.

Facing the entrance was a precipitous rocky background, where clear, spring water cascaded over mossy stones, maiden-hair and other ferns, flowing into a pond, encircled by tiles. Round about, slender pillars supported the balcony above, on to which the sleeping chambers opened.

It was a riot of color, where lively little brown-bodied lizards darted in and out of the foliage or sunned themselves on the parapet.

This spot could also have been a refuge when, with clear consciences, the family were able to escape the intense summer heat of Rome.

The banqueting hall in the west tower, now deserted, was a silent witness of ancient revelry. There were little lion faces, the empire furniture and empty chairs.

Across the courtyard east was the library; slender pillars soared to the ceiling, and between the arches were hung handsome curtains on poles. Oriental rugs were lavishly spread on marble floors. Flowering shrubs adorned this chamber. It was here fear-haunted hearts found sanctuary. Those fortunate to escape torture or death were nursed back to life, only perhaps to relive it at greater cost.

In a recess, Princess Claudia was writing. Many years had imprinted the passage of time, but she was still a very beautiful woman, with whom few could compete, and whom many envied.

She gazed languidly out of the broad window over the heads of slender cyress trees in the foreground, looking like dark fingers pointing upward in a straight and stiff row. Of what was she thinking as she held her quill pen suspended and her eyes roamed over the vast sweep of country beneath, where sun-baked towns and their graceful spires pierced the haze, the horizon fading into the sky?

Suddenly she leaned forward, for far below she noticed dust, and saw a lonely traveller. She wondered who it might be. Messengers were an unmixed pleasure and sorrow, for who knew what tidings they were burdened with.

"My eyes grow dim, and my heart is a sea of pain." Slowly she rolled up her manuscript and slipped it into the box.

She moved over the rugs in her matron's full robe, which now hung loosely on her once plump figure. She lingered by the pool and fed the fish, and slowly passed under the central arch on to the terrace, carrying a bunch of grapes.

"Whoever it is approaching will be glad of these"; and she laid them on a table where any who desired them could take what they needed. Then she sank on to her couch, and smiled as she saw her youngest daughter Praxedes waving to her from the end of the terrace.

On the edge of the parapet stood replicas of celebrated statues, and Praxedes had chosen to rest beneath Mercury, whose youthful form and winged feet could scarcely find a fitter spot to stand on, for he was in very truth poised in space.

Hearing snatches of song in the Podere, Praxedes rose and leaned over the balcony and watched the Vendemia, which was in full swing. The farmers were merry as they gathered the grapes. Women moved from tree to tree on which the vines grew, arrayed in gorgeous shawls and head kerchiefs of like brilliancy on their glossy dark hair.

Handsome debonair youths, with flashing eyes, flowers tucked over their ears, beneath which dangled huge earrings, sang popular snatches of love songs, directed for the most part towards some buxom maiden. For Italy, with its quaint ways, is to those who have seen her and learned to love her children, a pleasant possession and cherished memory.

A little apart, under some trees, stood the white cattle,

into happy youth before the anguish of the Infant Church in Rome had prematurely engraved sad and thoughtful lines on their young faces. Moreover, the arena might at any time claim their frail bodies.

In this dear Castello,' Princess Claudia and Praxedes were enjoying a brief visit to rest, and their guest was St. Paul. The others were in Rome.

Praxedes had been half asleep when she saw their benign visitor preparing to descend, so she bounded along the terrace, to join him, followed by her bleating nanny. The man who stirred the Eastern world folded his hand in prayer. At last she reached him, panting.

"Praxedes, beloved child, I beg you, carry this ink flask, lest it come to harm. I will then use my staff."

Together they slowly descended. Praxedes was unusually silent, and he saw the shadow of their farewell steal over her bright face.

They reached the terrace and advanced to where Princess Claudia was seated. She rose, smiling.

"Fair hostess, this is the last day of my visit; it has passed all too swiftly; and now I go to Rome, where I must finish and dispatch these letters."

Claudia moved to where he was sitting, while Praxedes prepared some fruit.

"Dear Father Paul, stay awhile; you are still so weary, and surely need more rest. You don't know what a privilege it is to have you with us. Alas! that Pudens is absent, but you know why —" Suddenly her face flushed and she said with unusual bitterness, "Christians are being slain like cattle, without trial. Truly our emperors have slain justice. And Nero ...!"

"God's servants, Claudia, cannot expect kinder treatment from Rome, who treated our King as they did.. Heaven is filling fast. But death – ah! wonderful thought and how much more a martyr's death is a painful but swift way of entering the portals of eternity. We must not wonder, beloved children," and he took Praxedes' hand, and read the deep mystery of her faithful heart chewing the cud, waiting for the order and a possible blow, when they had to lurch awkwardly forward, drawing the grape-ladened cart to the vats.

Praxedes contemplated this picturesque scene, and envied their happy hearts. Rome to them was but a name. A little bleating voice and soft nose made her turn, for her pet deer she had rescued wanted food, and it followed her like a dog.

Away in the curve of the hills frequented by the shepherdess and her flocks, and home of innumerable lizards, an elderly man was writing. He had cast aside his heavy Eastern draperies, now and again stroking his long thin beard. His pen moved slowly over the parchment letters destined to become precious to future generations, which were to be sent to the Churches in Asia and distant lands.

The sun having dried the ink, he carefully tied up the rolls with his slender fingers. He rose, and looking towards the castle, caught sight of Praxedes far off, waving to him.

He dearly loved the warm-hearted and impetuous girl, full of zeal for all that stood for noble and exalted ideals.

She appealed to him far more than her elder sister, Pudentiana, who was growing into a solid, solemn saint, now in Rome doing invaluable work superintending the philanthropic activities of the hospitium Apostolorum. Assisted by her brother, Timotheus, she had already commenced the work of laying out dead martyrs and bathing the wounds inflicted with such cruelty on those being tested almost beyond endurance rather than deny Him.

No, Pudentiana was most worthy. But really dull and heavy, she lacked the sparkle and fire her younger sister inherited from her Celtic forbears. But alas! Praxedes was saddened early, and was rapidly developing into a noble woman, for the great work which almost immediately was to demand her entire surrender.

Her mother's great sorrow was her inability to shield her from the days of terror that seemed to paralyze everyone, for no Christians could live in the days of Nero and not in some way share the sorrow of the Godhead.

The children of Pudens and Claudia had scarcely bloomed

in the gentle eyes that rested on his. He paused, momentarily startled, and passed his hand over is brow.

"No," he continued, "we must not marvel if we, too, have to experience some of His passion, for in these days the darkness of ignorance and heathenism is being greatly disturbed by the overwhelming light which is suddenly being turned on to old ideals from a new revelation."

Claudia meditatively said, "Yes! Pudens hovered uncertain. To him it was too ideal, except when he saw it working. But he was a Christian before either of us knew it; and since his conversion my marriage has been perfection."

Silence fell. Praxedes spoke in a low voice, "We cannot hope to escape the trials, Father Paul, nor would we. Pray for us."

"Praxedes, I see shadows over you; fear not, but tread bravely the days that lie ahead. Take them, and what they bring one by one. For each will need His strength for a cross or a crown."

"You know," she said. "God help me!"

"Dear children," said the tender-hearted man, "our lives are the tiny seeds sown in blood-moistened soil. Future generations will reap what may cost us life itself. Remember we are not living for these cloudy days, but for an eternal sunlit tomorrow. It is very near me — now — then forgiven, washed and reclothed, to be with Him forevermore."

ROMAN BRITAIN

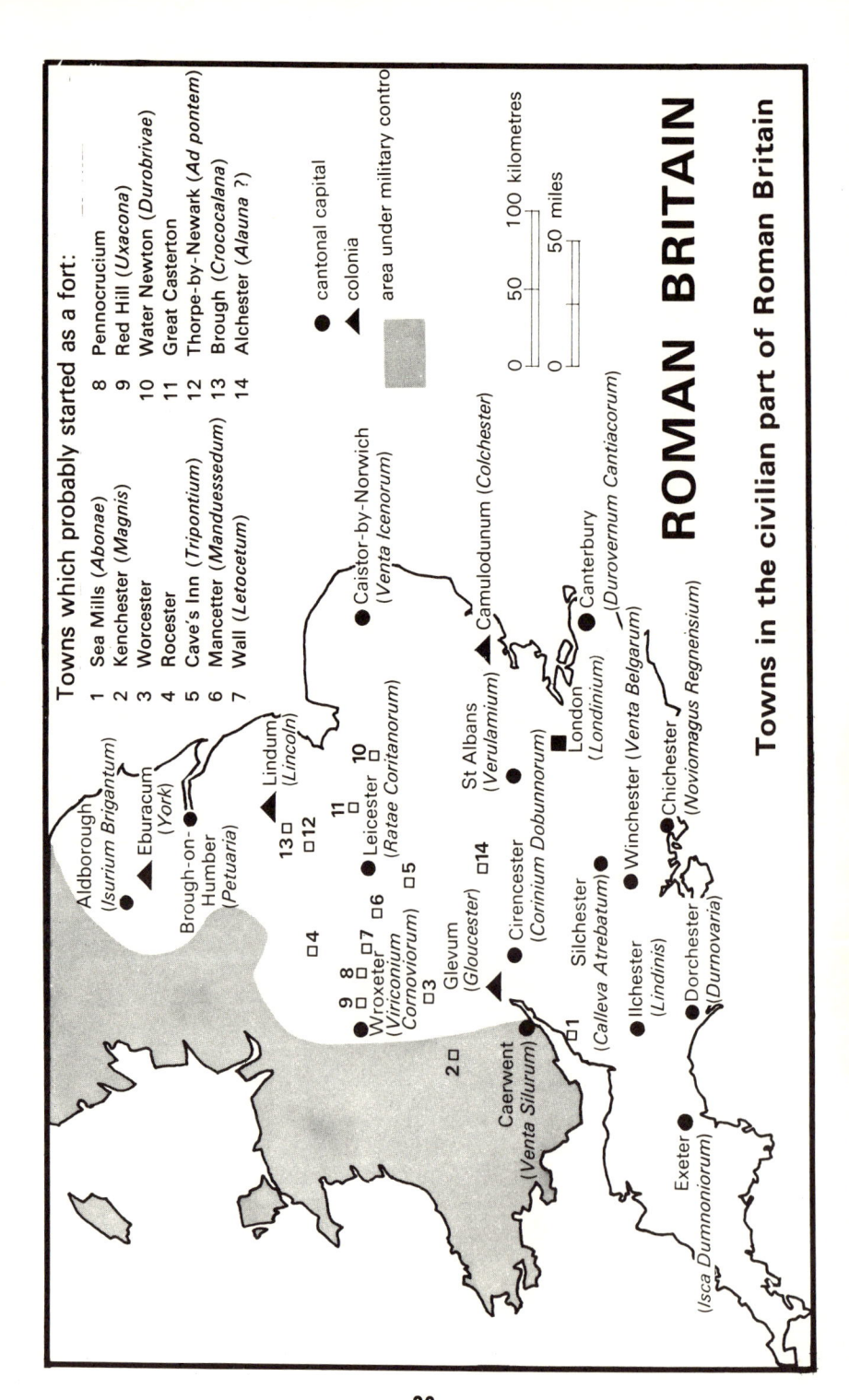

Towns in the civilian part of Roman Britain

Towns which probably started as a fort:

1. Sea Mills (*Abonae*)
2. Kenchester (*Magnis*)
3. Worcester
4. Rocester
5. Cave's Inn (*Tripontium*)
6. Mancetter (*Manduessedum*)
7. Wall (*Letocetum*)
8. Pennocrucium
9. Red Hill (*Uxacona*)
10. Water Newton (*Durobrivae*)
11. Great Casterton
12. Thorpe-by-Newark (*Ad pontem*)
13. Brough (*Crococalana*)
14. Alchester (*Alauna* ?)

- ● cantonal capital
- ▲ colonia
- ▬ area under military control

Towns shown:
- Aldborough (*Isurium Brigantum*)
- Eburacum (*York*)
- Brough-on-Humber (*Petuaria*)
- Lindum (*Lincoln*)
- Leicester (*Ratae Coritanorum*)
- Wroxeter (*Viroconium Cornoviorum*)
- Glevum (*Gloucester*)
- Cirencester (*Corinium Dobunnorum*)
- St Albans (*Verulamium*)
- Caistor-by-Norwich (*Venta Icenorum*)
- Camulodunum (*Colchester*)
- London (*Londinium*)
- Canterbury (*Durovernum Cantiacorum*)
- Silchester (*Calleva Atrebatum*)
- Winchester (*Venta Belgarum*)
- Chichester (*Noviomagus Regnensium*)
- Caerwent (*Venta Silurum*)
- Ilchester (*Lindinis*)
- Dorchester (*Durnovaria*)
- Exeter (*Isca Dumnoniorum*)

PART II

CHAPTER III

BISHOP LINUS (PRINCE LLEYN) A.D. 90

Rome was waking up after its midday siesta. The nobility refreshed, mounted their chariots, driven at high speed by drivers cruelly unheedful of the poor, the young, or aged, let alone rickety donkey carts laden with luscious fruits for the rich men's tables.

Here and there, weary ragged pedestrians with things that were once sandals tied to their feet by any old rag, pleaded in vain for charity; their pinched faces bespoke the misery of their empty stomachs. But what did the rich care for that which was written on their parchment skin drawn stiffly over their cheek-bones?

The youngest son of Senator Pudens, named Novatus, hurried through the crowded narrow street on his way to Palatium Apostolorum. The palace was a parting gift to Gladys and Senator Pudens, when King Caradoc returned to Britain. He reached the broad steps hot and dusty, with a sickly fear, glancing around him uneasily, trusting he would be in time to save the life so dear to them all, of Bishop Linus, his uncle. His footsteps echoed under the arched portico, and then into the peristyle, where tame doves were feeding, and quickly entered the apartment where the family was used to gathering.

Princess Claudia and his sisters were quietly occupied, much to his astonishment. His mother was alarmed at his sudden appearance, and dropping her quill pen, gazed in speechless wonder at her son with his panting short breaths, the dust of travel clinging to his raiment.

"What brings you here in such a condition, Novatus? Is anything wrong with your father?"

"No, dearest, he is well, but is it — Oh! how shall I say it? ... Is all well with Uncle Linus?"

Claudia started and clutched her heart. "What can it be, for no tidings have reached us, and you have travelled fast, perhaps on some false rumor. God grant it may be so." Pudentiana laid aside the wreath she was making, and the faint color fled, leaving her pallid. She moved over beside her mother, and took her hand, saying, "Dearest, I, too, have had great misgivings, for as I passed old Luigi at the Forum — and as you know he is usually a silent man — today he was speaking rapidly with a group of people.

"The name I heard caused my heart to faint within me, but without further confirmation I have hesitated to raise fears which perhaps are idle tales. Even now our Agatha is out to ascertain if it is really so. I heard words such as 'Down with the Christians,' 'the gods are angry!' "

"Behold Novatus," said Claudia, "the Atrium is prepared for a service, and we expect your uncle here at any moment."

As she spoke, they heard his voice chanting a hymn. A smiling face looked through the curtains, but a look of dismay and wonder appeared as he noted their tears.

"What's wrong, Claudia dearest? I do not understand." His great eyes, soft as gazelles', looked tenderly into the heart of the woman, the companion of his youth, who had been to him as a mother.

His tall form, slender yet strong hands, drew her limp form unresistantly to his heart, and he felt her trembling as she dropped her head on his shoulder.

He was calm — a man who had looked grim things in the face and had gained strength — and was able to help others in their life's crises. His position must have been an exceptionally difficult one in Rome.

His eyes looked around enquiringly and fell on Novatus in his travel-stained clothes.

"I think you are the source of this trouble, and bearer of ill tidings."

"Yes, uncle. I was working in the vineyard when Marcella approached me cautiously and whispered that ... Oh! ... how can I say it ...that Caesar has had a fresh list of Christians' names compiled." He gulped. Beads of perspiration oozed out through the dust on his forehead. "It is not too late for you, uncle, to leave Rome. I have thought of a place as I hurried here. It would spell disaster to the Church if anything happened to you; and I hoped to try to save ..."

"To save me, Novatus?" replied the bishop quickly.

"I am surprised at you, son of my heart, for this softness ill matches your own bravery; when your life trembled on the brink of death, your attitude was anything but soft. Your affection for me has carried you beyond a Christian's duty! Think, even if I am head of the flock here — a post entrusted to me by the beloved Apostles — could I relinquish it? Never! and certainly not to save my life! How could I?" he asked, human love and affection surging up, causing a catch in his voice he was unable to steady, "Forsake this work? I would be an unworthy follower of the Master if I did. My life is His; if he needs me here, no harm will befall me. Or if martyrdom is to His greater glory, well, I am ready."

The words were still on his lips when a scared attendant ushered in a heavily-cloaked man, his face hidden.

"Who are you who fears to show his face?" asked the Bishop.

The man scattered sand on the pavement and, stooping, drew the Christian's symbol. As he rose his cloak slipped to the ground and they saw a Roman soldier, his helmet tucked under his arm. They stared, amazed, as he stood so silently in their midst.

"Speak, servant of Caesar, and tell us why you have drawn a cross?" asked the bishop.

"Noble Prince from 'The Island of the Mighty' " — they started momentarily and looked at each other wonderingly — "Forgive, I pray you, this hasty visit, but I am under military orders. Here is an official roll for you, Bishop Linus," and he commenced to detach it from his belt.

"This contains the Emperor's wishes and royal command, which must be obeyed. Soldiers follow hard on my heels to arrest you in Caesar's name. To me alas, has been entrusted this hateful office, and it is only part of what I deserve. Listen all of you, for there is yet time. You, O Bishop, represent the heart of Christianity in Rome. The decree has gone forth that this faith must be broken up; it is loathed. It claims too many of the flower of our nation, it upsets the Senators and patricians when their staffs refuse to attend the temple rites, and openly defy their masters. Too many, they say, are deserting the gods. It is a grievous offense in this realm." He paused, they were too stunned to utter.

"I seem to remember your face. But where have we met before?" asked the bishop.

"Noble Prince, I was in Siluria, and helped to capture your noble father, King Caradoc, to his undoing. I carried the fatal letter which Queen Cartismandua entrusted to General Ostorius Scapula. He was ever striving to shield his own skin, and cared little for the danger which lay about my path, as I carried that invitation he feared to handle to our King Caradoc." A slight noise caused him to peer nervously into the shadows. "That Brigantine Queen was no friend to your father, and now Ostorius, (It is possible General Ostorius Scapula had died before this date.) weary of British valor, is by his own desire here in Rome. I hate him! He bribed me to carry out what he feared to do himself, so that any punishment would fall on me. I am a nervous man, but he is a bigger coward than I am," he remarked bitterly. "He inspired me with false hopes and promise of abundant wealth. Gold coins flowed into his pouch, mine remained empty. My only reward was to act as jailer to the noble Paul, as you all know."

The others looked at him keenly. "He was confined in one of the worst cells in the Marmertine, dripping with moisture, where no warm sunbeams penetrated. He languished for months, growing thinner and thinner. I did what I could. I carried in warm, dry straw, and shared my flask of wine and my bread with him.

"In the flickering torchlight his face was wonderfully bright, and he was as affectionate as any woman. We listened to the animals within a few paces from his cell fighting over their frugal fare; they are kept half starved in the arena." The soldier paused and looked around at them all.

"Then he told me about the Saviour, and how He came down from heaven to live as man and died for man's sin, and that I, too, might live with Him after death if I would believe and repent. Oh! how brave he was; so uncomplaining; all because he reproved the Emperor and hated our gods and monuments. We had many talks.

"Do you think that I stood forth in gratitude to God? For I had learned to believe, and in my heart was a Christian. No, I hid and avoided your people on every occasion. I sought the shade of friendly walls during the services, longing to join, with no courage to openly face the consequences. I am as vile a coward as ever trod this earth," and he sank on his knees before the bishop.

"I am here to confess all this and the injury I did to you and yours years ago in Siluria."

"No, Marco," said the princess, "it was God's plan. We are not living in Rome for naught. Some day we shall know."

Marco rose and gazed wonderingly at her and said, "It was when I heard that Caesar had orders to arrest Prince Linus, the bishop, and that he was a doomed man, did I shake myself together. I faced my cringing self; I couldn't sleep. A fever of consuming unrest ate up my heart. I wrestled as any gladiator, only with myself. At last in grief I told God everything. I tried to think your Saviour was really before me. Now I am at peace. I care not what my fate is to be. I live to die, in the arena, or as my Emperor and his cruel servants decide. I should be glad now to witness with a courage I never before possessed. Pray I may be faithful, come what may, to the Crucified. I have joined his army, and it needed some courage."

They heard heavy footsteps approaching; their eyes searched the shadowy columns. They beheld a tall, powerful Roman, striding along as if the palace belonged to him. Each footfall fell as a hammer blow of terror on their quivering anxious hearts.

The faint moon, still low, glinted from his armor as he passed pillar after pillar; his helmet brushed the palms. As he saw them he halted, his beetling brows knit together over his cruel eyes, luridly glancing from one to another. He folded his arms, knotted with muscles like cords. His lips were drawn back with a triumphant sneering smile over his decayed teeth, giving him a distinctly canine look.

"Why do you enter this way?" asked the bishop.

"I enter by Caesar's order!"

"Your name, general?" A loud mirthless laugh rang out.

"You ask my name, O Prince! It is famous in the Britainic Isles, as here in Caesar's city, proud Mistress of the Tiber. Before you stands General Ostorius Scapula. Hah! hah! That's something to make you remember 'The Island of the Mighty.' And what a misnomer! I am a maker of history; my name will be remembered long after I am dead," and he beat his chest, which sounded as empty as a drum. He swung his well-filled pouch; "and when this is empty I remind the Emperor of my exploits in the 'Cheerless Isle.' "

He raised his hand, pointing to the bishop, and said: "How are the mighty fallen." Then he swung round toward Claudia, "It was I who captured Rome's toughest enemy, the British lion, the far-famed so-called barbarian! But with mighty fine claws! A chief — puff!" He bowed aggressively towards Claudia, "and your charming sister, Lleyn, is ..."

"Silence!" commanded the bishop. "Your speech is odious — your duty lies with me."

Ostorius, with danger hatred, and furiously angry at being reproved, strode towards his victum and in a cruel tone said: 'You will have good reason to remember me, Llyen, and before I have finished with you — you will have drawn your last breath."

Princess Claudia swayed. Pudentiana and Praxedes supported their mother, encouraging her to be brave.

Ostorious, scowling at Marco, drew his sword and pricked his leg. "Awake, Marco!" For he was intently looking at the princess, vividly remembering her luxurious auburn hair as it caught the sunbeams when he seized her in the quarry, and now it was white, and she was changed, nearing her three score years.

"Marco, you have not delivered the Emperor's letter to the bishop"; and he struck him with his sword across the shoulders. "You continue ever slack, I perceive. For this you must be punished, but for you, the lions are too gentle. Your death-bed would be soft indeed tied to the royal chariot wheel as Caesar enters the emporium! I will have no Christians among my soldiers!"

The bishop read Caesar's letter. Silence was broken by the ominous tramp of heavy feet advancing, clanking swords, loud voices, until the glittering spearheads protruded above the heavy draperies that curtained off this part of the palace from the courtyard.

"I am ready," said the bishop, handing back the roll. "I ask one kind concession, namely a few minutes alone with my relatives. I beg therefore you will leave us."

Ostorius Scapula, at the point of his sword, would have driven out Marco, who was staunching the wound in his leg, but the bishop laid his hand on the young convert and said, "No, my son; your duty to the Emperor is ended. Your place now is by my side to live or die as a Christian. Let us pray."

They sank on their knees, hearts too full for words, while the bishop on the eve of his martyrdom prayed for them all, and the work of the Church he was leaving.

Marco lifted the bishop's hand and pressed his lips to it. The bishop gave a blessing to the trembling Roman, and silently they committed themselves to the Almighty God.

The last heart-breaking farewells had ended as a voice from outside said, "The arena larder needs replenishing. Caesar's wild animals are starving."

The moonlight shone fitfully; the shadows turned blue as the licentious and idolatrous city grew quiet, except for some riotous youths returning from, or going to, late banquets, to become craven slaves of wine and women. Drunken slumberers lay on soft silken divans.

In the magnificent temples the watchful vestal virgins fanned the alter fires. Thin threads of smoke quivered uncertainly in the still air.

Today some of those elegant buildings stand, weather worn, but still beautiful, although white with age.

The Coliseum, too, ruined but awesome, where gladiatorial games, chariot races, and, worse still, scenes of unmerited cruelty to Christians took place.

Why rewrite the horrors that beset the Infant Faith in the

first and second centuries, staining the pages of Italy's pagan and religious life?

The emperors knew no god but the gods. Not so the great Church which was nourished on its soil and caused the death of innumerable Christians.

We are concerned with the fate of one family. Yet victims for Christ all over the continent, and not Rome alone, together with other religious bodies, have caused a mountainous pile of dead. This demonstrates how the fundamental doctrines of Christianity became the target of Satan — inspired, so-called Christian enthusiasts shooting deadly weapons at co-religionists, who differ from the views. Misguided, self-aggressiveness! Christians turned into murderers! Amazing!

Torches smirched and flared under the trees, as a sad procession reached "the spur of the Aventine," which overlooks the Circus of Maximus, where the catacombe "di s. Calisto casa di Aquila e Pricilla" (of St. Calisto, house of Aquila and Pricilla) was — carrying the loving hearted prince bishop of noble ancestry to his resting-place.

It is thought he lies in St. Peter's cathedral, not far from the great Apostle.

Linus, first Bishop of Rome, was the first of his family to suffer martyrdom in A.D. 90.

Irenaeus writes, A.D. 190, "The Apostles, having founded and built up the Church at Rome, committed the ministry and its supervision to Linus. This Linus is mentioned by Paul in his Epistles to Timothy."

It may seem a dismal ending. Remember this is no romance of imaginary people whose life stories are brain creations, concluding with long separated lovers, reunited to live hereafter happily.

This is a glimpse into old European history, out of whose meager details the life story of this Welsh and illustrious royal family has been reconstructed.

Let us not forget that they are our own race, that they drank from the same springwater on our hillsides; that they trod the hills and valleys of Cambria, and gathered as we do the whin-berries on the heathery moorland hedges.

Let us, in spite of contrary assertions of priority, remember with gratitude and treasure our apostolically built Church, a rich inheritance, for none can dispute our claim to being as Fuller says, *"The senior Church of the world."*

Documentary evidence is too abundant and sure, and too well known and confirmed to be questioned.

"The Church of Avalon in Britain no other hands than those of the disciples of the Lord themselves built," while St. Joseph of Arimathaea, Simon Zelotes, Bishop Aristobulus, and, as many believe, St. Paul himself, were in Britain.

Rome had interests in Palestine, as it was barely twenty years since Titus conquered and desecrated the Holy City.

The British family, under the providence of God, protected those who had seen and spoken to our Lord personally.

Wealthy, their home became the center where Christians from the West met Christians from the East.

It is good, surely, to remember their lives.

The Nobility of Eternity!

"Faith of our Father's! living still
In spite of dungeon, fire and sword:
O how our hearts beat high with joy,
Whene'er we hear that glorious word.
  Faith of our Fathers! Holy Faith!
  We will be true to Thee till death."

"Our Fathers chained in prisons dark,
Were still in heart and conscience free,
How sweet would be their children's fate,
If they, like them, could die for Thee!
  Faith of our Fathers, etc."

F.W. Faber

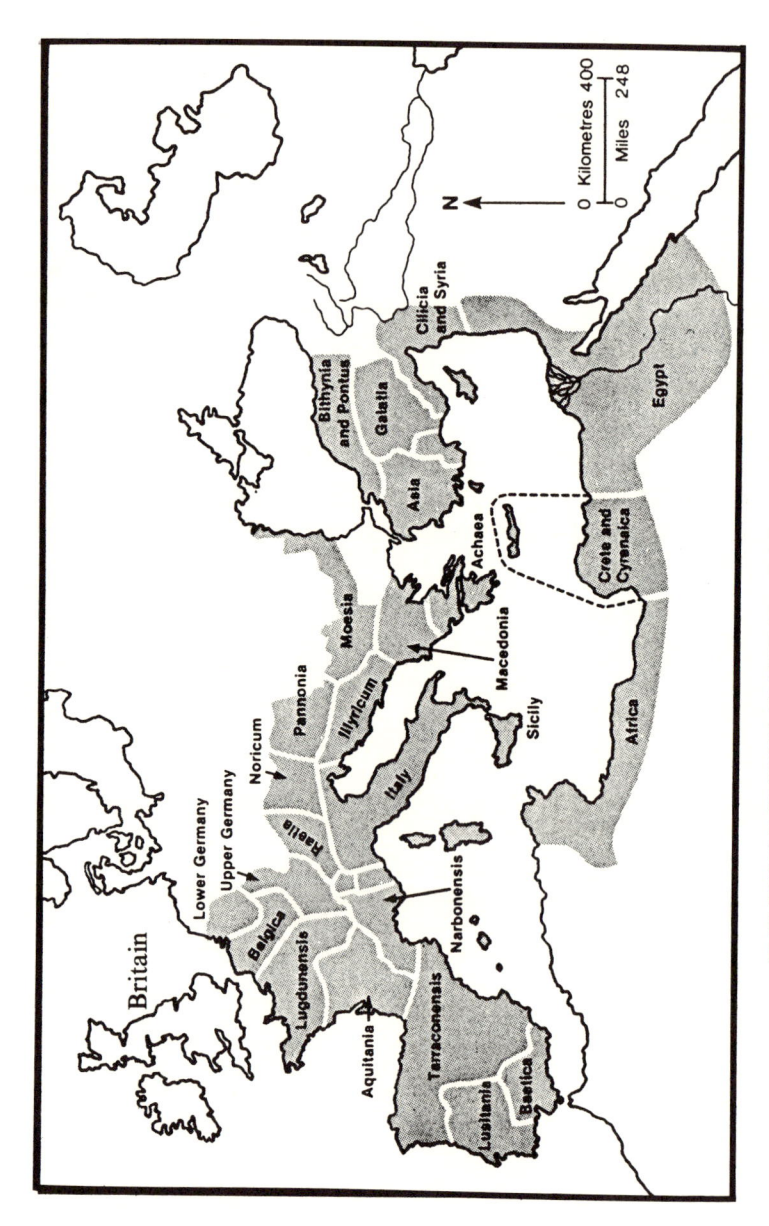

THE ROMAN EMPIRE AT THE TIME OF ST. PAUL'S JOURNEYS.

PART III

NOTES FOR REFERENCE

1. St. Paul in Britain.
2. St. Aristobulus, first British bishop (Morgan).
3. Prince—Bishop—Lleyn—Linus; extract from "Lives of the Saints" (Baring-Gould). Extract from "St. Paul in Britain."
4. Rufus Pudens Pudentius and Princess Claudia
5. King Caradoc Pendragon—Caractacus and his palace—Llantwit Major, Glamorganshire.
6. The Titulus. Lanciani's "Pagan and Christian Rome."
7. Form of Divine Service. Notes from "Early Christian Art."
8. "Wells and Glastonbury Abbey" (Scott Holmes).
9. "Victims of the Marmertine" (O'Reilly).
10. "Queen Elizabeth and Glastonbury."

ST. PAUL IN BRITAIN

Theodoret, writing A.D. 435 (born 390), Bishop of Cyrus, near Antioch, in Syria, said: "Paul, liberated from his first captivity at Rome, preached the gospel to the Britons and others in the West. Our fishermen and publicans not only persuaded the Romans and their tributaries to acknowledge the Crucified and His Laws, but the Britons also and the Cymry."

In his commentary on 2 Tim. iv. 16:

"When Paul was sent by Festus on his appeal to Rome, he travelled, after being acquitted, into Spain, and thence extended his excursions into other countries and the isles surrounded by the sea."

Chrysostom, Patriarch of Constantinople, supplies (A.D. 402) cumulative evidence of the existence of pure British Christianity. "The British Isles," he writes, "which are beyond the sea and which lie in the ocean, have received the virtue of the Word. Churches are there founded and altars erected."

"Though thou shouldst hear all men everywhere discoursing matters out of the Scriptures, with another voice, indeed, but not another faith, with a different tongue, but the same judgment."

Eusebius, in A.D. 320, Bishop of Caesarea, speaks of Apostolic Missions to Britain as matter of notoriety. "The Apostles passed beyond the ocean and the isles called the Britannic Isles" (Page 172)

"St. Paul lived, according to all evidence, whenever he was in Rome, whether in custody, at large (libra custodia) or free, in the bosom of the Claudian family."

But *Clemens Romanus* not only proves to us that the family which the Apostle thus honored with his constant residence and instruction was British, that the first bishop appointed by him over the Church at Rome was of this British family, but that St. Paul himself preached in Britain, for not other interpretation can be assigned to his words (Greek) "the extremity of the West."

Page 175. "There are six years of St. Paul's life to be accounted for between his liberation from his first imprisonment and his martyrdom, at Aquae Salviae in the Ostian Road, near Rome.

"Part, certainly the greater part perhaps, of this period was spent in Britain — in Siluria or Cambria, beyond the bounds of the Roman Empire, and hence the silence of the Greek and Latin writers upon it."

[Footnote: "The ancient MS. in Merton College, Oxford, which purports to contain a series of letters between St. Paul and Seneca, has more than one allusion to St. Paul's residence in Siluria."]

There are "Ancient British Triads: Triads of St. Paul the Apostle" (page 177).

"The foundation of the great Abbey of Bangor Iscoed is assigned by tradition to St. Paul. Its discipline and doctrine were known as 'the Rule of Paul' (Pauli Regula), and over each of the four gates was engraved his precept: 'If a man will not work, neither let him eat.' "

Page 170. Interred "in Via Ostiensis." [Footnote (page 177): "Pelagius heresiarchus ex Britannia oriundus famati illius collegii Bangorensis praepositus eiat in quo Christianorum philosophorum 2,100 militabant suarum manum laboribus juxta Pauli doctrinam victitantes." Vita Pelagii p. 3.]

Morgan

ST. ARISTOBULUS

Extracts from "St. Paul in Britain" (Morgan),

Page 131.

"It is perfectly certain," writes Alford, "that before St. Paul had come to Rome, Aristobulus was absent in Britain."

We have seen he was not at Rome when Paul wrote his Epistle. Now, Aristobulus must have been far advanced in years, for he was the father-in-law of St. Peter. His wife was the subject of the miracle recorded by St. Matthew.

We have the following evidences that he preached the Gospel and was martyred in Britain: *The martyrologies of the Greek Churches.*

Aristobulus was one of the seventy disciples, and a follower of St. Paul the Apostle. He was chosen by St. Paul to be the missionary bishop to the land of Britain, a very warlike and fierce race. By them he was often scourged and repeatedly dragged as a criminal through their towns; yet he converted many of them to Christianity. He was there martyred, after he had built churches and ordained deacons and priests for the island. (Greek men, Ad 15 March.)

Haleca, Bishop of Augusta, to the same effect: "The memory of many martyrs is celebrated by the Britons, especially that of St. Aristobulus, one of the seventy disciples." (Halecae Fragments martyr.)

Adonis Martyrologia: Natal Day of Aristobulus, Bishop of Britain, brother of St. Barnabus, the Apostle, by whom he was ordained bishop. He was sent to Britain, where, after preaching the truth of Christ and forming a Church, he received martyrdom. (In Diem Martii 17.)

The British Achu, or genealogies of the Saints of Britain: "There came with Bran the Blessed, from Rome to Britain, Arwystli Hen (Senex) Ilid Cyndaw, men of Israel or Manaw, son of Arwystli Hen." (Achan Saint Prydain.)

According to the genius of the British tongue, Aristobulus becomes Arwystli. A district in Montgomeryshire on the Severn perpetuates by its name Arwystli in person among them they must have been struck with the age of the venerable missionary or the epithet Senex would not have become amongst them part of his name.

Further evidence is to be found in St. George's Church, Fordington "Monthly Messenger"

March 1908 Vicar's Letter.
The Rev. H. Grovenor Bartelot, M.A.
Bishop Aristobulus (First Bishop of Britain)

"On February 5th, in the course of our restoration work, we discovered that great block of stone which figures as our illustration in this month's "Messenger." The bishop came to see it and made a minute examination and a tracing of it. Copies have been sent to the British Museum and elsewhere, to expert Romanologists ... First of all ... the slab of Purbeck marble is 2 ft. 11 inches by 2 ft. 4½ inches, and 6 inches thick.

It is thus inscribed — the mark -/- indicating letters which are worn away by age:

G-ARI-/-/—/-/-
CIVI-/-OM-/-
AN-/-L
RVFIN VS ET
-/—/-ARINA ET
AVILA-FILI EIVS
E-ROMANA VXO-/-

Now, what is the meaning of those letters? They evidently commemorate some Roman of ancient days, and he must have been a person of importance... Unfortunately, at least ten letters are lost ... Still, what remains we can translate it as follows and let experts have their say afterwards:

To Gais Ari (stolus?)
A Roman Citizen
Aged 50 years
Rufinus and
Marina and Avea his children
by Romana his wife, etc. etc.

The name Rufinus suggests a most interesting sequence of thought which carries us back, not only to Roman society of the first century, but even to St. Paul himself, and to the early Christian converts.

. . . .

It is a significant fact that the Greek historian, Eusebius, states that Britain owed its Christianity to some of the Apostles, and, moreover, the great Menologies tell us that:

"Aristobulus, the divine Apostle of Christ, was one of the seventy disciples ... and when Paul ordained bishops in every country he ordained Aristobulus bishop in the country of the Britons — who were unbelievers and rude and fierce men — and he departed thither and at other times being dragged through the streets, and again at other times derided, persuaded many to turn to Christ and to be baptised; and he founded churches and appointed priests and deacons, and there he died."

Another account says that he died in the year A.D. 99, and was buried at Glastonbury, and his day was kept on March 15th. The Welsh traditions also describe how Aristobulus (Arwystli Hen) came from Rome as a missionary to Britain, accompanying the family of Caractacus on their return from captivity, certain Jews (Judeans) named Ilid and Cyndav and Mawan his son were their companions. The question then is, have we not here at St. George's the identical tombstone of Aristobulus himself, the first Apostle to our land? The fact that he is stated to be buried at Glastonbury is a matter of no concern, for there was no Roman town at Glastonbury, and not until years after the first century were the bones of the saints removed for safety to that sacred spot when the heathen invaders came across the seas.

"... For eighteen centuries a religious, if not a Christian building, has rendered sacred the site of our Church of St. George ... Our stone weighs nearly a quarter of a ton. It has been a very sacred stone, one which the Britons buried for safety when the Saxons invaded our shores. It never suffered from exposure until Normans erected their celebrated tympanum with St. George fighting for England. They found that the tympanum necessitated a porch, so they turned the tablet face downwards and made it the foundation stone for their porch; but there it would not stand the weight, it cracked in two, the roots of plants were growing out of the crack when the restoration of the twentieth century brought to light this most wonderful relic of ancient Fordington."

PRINCE — BISHOP — LLEYN — LINUS
2 Tim. iv. 21.

Extract from the Rev. S. Baring Gould's "Lives of the Saints":

"Linus, a Christian at Rome, known to St. Paul and St. Timothy, is asserted unequivocally by Trenaeus to have been the first Bishop of Rome. Eusebius and Theodoret corroborate this statement and all ancient writers agree that the first Bishop of Rome after the Apostles was named Linus. The date of his appointment and duration of his Episcopate and the limits to which his Episcopal authority extend are points which cannot be regarded as absolutely settled, though they have been discussed at great length.

"Eusebius and Theodoret state that he became Bishop of Rome after the death of St. Peter. On the other hand, the words of Irenaeus — 'When they founded and built up the church (of Rome) committed the office of its Episcopate to Linus' — certainly admit, or rather imply, the meaning that he held office *before* the death of St. Peter. The duration of his Episcopate is given by Eusebius as A.D. 68-80, but there are difficulties in the way of accepting these dates."

Page 171. "Have we any direct contemporary evidence the first Bishop of Rome was the son of Caractacus, a brother of Claudia Britannica? Does any contemporary of St. Paul and Linus in Rome itself assert the fact? Undoubtedly. Clemens Romanus, who is mentioned by St. Paul, states in his Epistle, the genuineness of which has never been questioned, that Linus was the brother of Claudia. 'Sanctissimus Linus frater Claudia.'

"Clemens succeeded Cletus within twelve years of the death of Linus as third Bishop of Rome. Concerning those bishops who have been ordained in our lifetime, we make known to you that they are these: of Antioch, Euodius, ordained by me, Peter; of the church of Rome, Linus, the (son) of Claudia first ordained by Paul and after Linus' death Clemens the second ordained by me, Peter."

"The Apostles," writes Irenaeus, A.D. 180, "having founded and built up the Church at Rome, committed the ministry of its supervision to Linus."

Apostolici constitutiones, c. 46.

The Apostolic constitutions may or may not be what their present title infers, but no scholar who peruses the opinions pro et contra collected by Iligius "(De Patribus Apostolicis), Buddaeus (Isagoge in Theologiam), and Baratier (De successione Grimorum Episcoporum), will assign them a later date than A.D. 150."

Extract from Lanciani's "Pagan and Christian Rome."

Page 130. "In St. Peter's Cathedral."

"Memoria sacre delle sette chiesa di roma, written by Giovanni Severano, p. 20.

"In 1615, when Paul V built the stairs leading to the Confession in the crypts, several bodies were found lying in coffins tied with linen bands ... one of the coffins bore, however, the name Linus."

It proceeds to say that Linus "was buried side by side with the remains of the blessed Peter in the Vatican Oct. 24." Even if we were disposed to doubt Torrigio's correctness in copying the name of the second Bishop of Rome, the fact of his burial in this place seems to be certain, because: "Heabanus Maurus, a poet in the ninth century, speaks of Linus' tomb as visible and accessible in the year 822."

RUFUS PUDENS PUDENTIUS
(Senator)

Rufus Pudens Pudentius was stationed by Aulus Plautius as praetor Castrorum at Regnum. (Chichester)

We possess in Chichester Museum a remarkably interesting monument of the residence of Pudens in this city.

.   .   .   .

In the year A.D. 1723, while excavating the foundations of some houses, the monument to which we refer, generally known as the Chichester stone, was discovered. The inscription, which was partly mutilated and is cut in very bold characters, as restored by Horsley and Gale is as follows:

> NEPTUNO ET MINERVAE
> TEMPLUM
> PRO SALUTE DOMUS DIVINAE
> EX AUCTORITATE TIB CLAUDII
> COGIDUNI REGIS LEGATI AUGUSTI
> IN BRITANNIA
> COLLEGIUM FABRORUM ET QUI IN
> EO DONANTE AREAM PUDENTE
> PUDENTINI FILIO

"The attachment between Pudens and Claudia (Gladys, King Caradoc's youngest daughter, renamed Claudia) first grew up when the former was stationed Regnum.

"Their marriage took place in the 'first Christian church at Rome, known as the 'Titulus,' and now as St. Pudentiana.

"Here the nuptials of Claudia and Rufus Pudens Pudentius were celebrated in A.D. 53.

"Claudia was born A.D. 36, and at her marriage with Rufus was in her seventeenth year ... Claudia wrote several volumes of odes and hymns ... The palace of the British king formed a rendezvous for poets and authors of Rome" (i.e. Hospitium Britannicum). "Some conception of its size and magnificence from the number of servants ... as we learn from the Roman Martyrology, were two hundred males, and the same number of females, all born on the hereditary estates of Pudens, in Umbria."

Footnote:

"Adjacent to the palace (Umbria) were baths on a corresponding scale, known subsequently as Thermae Timothinae and Thermae Novatinae. The palace and ground were bequeathed by Timotheus to the Church at Rome — and these were the only buildings of any magnitude possessed by the Roman Church till the reign of Constantine."

Footnote:

"Claudia was the first hostess or harborer of St. Peter and St. Paul at the time of their coming to Rome."

Parsons "Three Conversions of England," Vol. I, p. 16.

"The children of Claudia and Pudens, as we learn from the Roman Martyrologies, were brought up on his knees" (i.e. St. Paul's).

THE BRITISH ROYAL FAMILY NATAL DAYS

Linus, Nov. 26th A.D. 90.

Pudens, A.D. 96.

Pudentiana suffered on the anniversary of her father's martyrdom in the third persecution, A.D. 107.

Novatus in the fifth persecution, A.D. 139, when his brother Timotheus was absent in Britain, baptizing his nephew King Lucius.

Timotheus suffered with his fellow-soldier Marcus, ... shortly after his return from Britain in extreme old age, about his ninetieth year.

Praxedes, the surviving sister, received her crown within the same year.

They were all interred by the side of St. Paul in the Via Ostiensis.

MORGAN

KING CARADOC (CARACTACUS) PENDRAGON
"St. Paul in Britain" (Morgan)

Page 88. "Caractacus was born at Trevran, the seat of his father Bran, within the present parish of Llanilid, in Glamorganshire. He received his education at the Druidic cor of Caerleon-on-Usk, where most of the Silurian nobility were trained in the cycle of Celtic accomplishments."

Page 135. Bran Arch-Druid of Caerleon-on-Usk. "It appears that Bran left Rome with Aristobulus and his son Manaw, Ilid, and Cyndaw, before Caradoc. He was accompanied also by Eurgain, the eldest daughter of Caradoc, and her husband Salog — lord in his right of Caer Salog (Salisbury), a Roman patrician.

"Ilid established his mission under the protection of Bran; his grandson Cyllinus (eldest son of Caradoc) Salog and Eurgain, in the centre of Siluria, on the spot in Glamorganshire known from that period till the present as Llan-Ilid.

"At this Llan, 'or consecrated enclosure', the Princess Eurgain founded and endowed the first Christian cor, or choir, in Britain. From this cor, Eurgain, issued many of the most eminent teachers and missionaries of Christianity down to the tenth century. Of the saints of this cor, from Ilid in succession, there are cataloges in the 'Genealogies of the Saints of Britain.'

"King Caradoc returned to Britain after seven years detention in Rome.

"Caractacus continued to reside at Aber Gweryd, now St. Donat's Major (Llan Daunwyd), in Glamorganshire, where he had built a palace, More Romano."

In the *National Message* (September 20th, 1930) is an article by R. Mayell — with reference to a party of sightseers to that neighborhood, so closely touching the illustrious royalties of Siluria.

"*Llantwit Major, Glamorganshire* ... That old world town nestling among the dunes on the north bank of the Bristol Channel between Cardiff and Swansea. Near by at St. Donats lie the ruins of the palace of Caradoc, ancient Britain's best known king (now in charge of Mr. Hearst of U.S.A.).

.   .   .   .   .

"We listened to our guide, Rev. J. W. Evans, as he graphically described Caradoc's journey to Rome; the romantic courtship of his daughter Gladys to the Roman officer, Pudens, and how natural it seemed that, when the royal party returned to the royal palace here at St. Donats, St. Paul should be one of the party, and later on preach on the spot in the town now marked by a cross. And also that before his return a college should be erected, part of the walls of which may now be seen, which pre-dates the University of Alexandria.

"Among the students were St. Illtitus and St. David, Gildas the historian and the great St. Patrick.

"This centre of learning still persists in the present Cowbridge High School close by.

"Later we visited the seashore; when the tide is very low may be seen the black relics of an ancient landing stage, where possibly the royal party and Paul landed."

Extract from private letter:

"King Caradoc's palace ruins are near St. Donats Castle. The owner who had the things covered over was a Mr. Loder Vachel ... The tesselated floor, with rider in full dress, is under a field now.

"When these things were discovered, a private view of them was given to some notables, including royalty, I believe, to which the owner of the land was not invited — he ordered everything to be covered over again. This was about thirty-seven to forty years ago. The field where the relics are leads to another residence, called "Dimlands," and another half mile further on is St. Donats Castle, a very old royal residence facing the sea, with battlements in front, where a regiment of soldiers was kept. There is a station at Llantwit Major. The footpath where the ruins are can be recognized by various mounds."

LANCIANI'S "PAGAN AND CHRISTIAN ROME"
The "Titulus"

"Rooms of private houses where the first prayer meetings were held ... bear in mind early Christian edifices in Rome ..." (were named) "from their founder or owner."

Private oratories "The upper chamber." Rome possesses remains the hours of prayer in which the Gospel was first announced in Apostolic times.

Five names in connection with the visit of St. Peter and Paul to the capitol of the empire, and two houses are mentioned as those in which they found hospitality; and were able to preach the new doctrine. One of these belong to Pudens and his daughters Pudentiana and Praxedes; stands half way up the Vicus Patricius (Via del Bambin Gesu) on the southern slope of the Viminal, and the other to Aquella and Prisca (or Pricilla), on the spur of the Aventine, which overlooks the Circus Maximus.

Both have been represented now by a church named after the owner, the Titulus Pudentis, and the Titulus Priscae.

Archaeologists have tried to trace the genealogy of Pudens, the friend of the Apostles, but although it seems probable that he belonged to the noble race of the Cornelii Aemilii, the fact has not yet been proved.

In the excavations of 1776 was found a bronze tablet which had been offered to Gaius Marcus Pudens Cornelianus by the people of Clunia (near Valencia, Spain, as a token of gratitude for the services he had rendered them during his governorship ... The tablet ... proves that the house owned by Aquela and Prisca in Apostolic times had subsequently passed into the hand of a Cornelius Pudens; in other words, that the relationship between the two families during the sojourn of the Apostles in Rome had been faithfully maintained by their descendants.

Their intimate connection is also proved by the fact that Pudens, Pudentiana, Praxedes and Prisca, were all buried in the same cemetery of Pricilla on the Via Salaria.

A very old tradition confirmed by the "Libre Pontificalis" describes the modern Church of St. Pudentiana as having been once the private house of the same Pudens, who was baptised by the Apostles and who is mentioned in the Epistle of St. Paul. Here the first converts met for prayers; here Pudentiana and Praxedes and Timotheus, daughters and son of Pudens, obtained from Pias I the institution of a regular parish assembly (Titulus) provided with a baptismal font, and here for a long time were preserved some pieces of household furniture which had been used by St. Peter. The tradition deserves attention, because it was openly accepted at the beginning of the fourth century. The name of the church at that time was simply "Ecclesia Pudentiana" which means "the Church of Pudens," its owner and founder.

An inscription discovered by Lelio Pasqualini speaks of a Leopadus, lector de Pudentiana in the year 384; and in the mosaic of the apse the Redeemer holds a book, on the open page of which is written: "The Lord the defender of the Church of Pudens ..."

Ignorant people changed the word Pudentiana, a possessive adjective, into the name of a saint, and the name of Sancta Pudentiana usurped the place of the genuine one. It appears for the first time in a document of the year 745.

The connection of the house with the Apostolate of SS. Peter and Paul made it very popular from the beginning; laymen and clergy alike contributed to transform it into a handsome church.

The remains of the house of Pudens were found in 1870. They occupy a considerable area under the neighboring houses.

The theory accepted by some modern writers as regards the transformation of these halls into regular churches is as follows:

The prayer meetings were held in the tablinum, or reception room of the house, which, as shown in the accompanying plan, opened on the atrium, or court (B), or this was surrounded by a portico or peristyle (C). In the early days of the Gospel the tablium could easily accommodate a small congregation of converts, but as this increased in numbers the space became inadequate, and the faithful were compelled to occupy the section of the portico which was in front of the meeting hall.

When the congregation grew larger there was no other way than by covering it with an awning or roof.

The tablinum became an Apse; the court roofed over became the nave; the side wings of the peristyle became aisles.

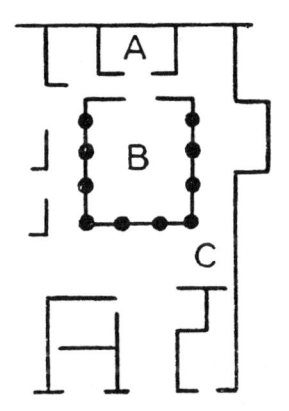

A. Tablinum.
B. Court.
C. Peristyle

The Church Itself.
The Titulus.

On its walls is attached a tablet, which translated reads as follows:

"In this sacred and most ancient of churches known as that of the Pastor, dedicated by Santus Pias Papa, formerly the house of the Holy Apostles, repose the remains of three thousand blessed martyrs, which Pudentiana and Praxedes, Virgins of Christ, with their own hands interred.

"The Confirmation of the Holy Pope is valuable as giving official Roman confirmation on the spot."

NOTES FROM "EARLY CHRISTIAN ART" BY EDWARD N. CULTS
Form of Divine Service

Page 7, etc. — "The early morning assembly for the Breaking of Bread ... some furniture is required, at least a plate for the bread, a cup for the wine, a table to place them upon ... The well-to-do, instead of keeping precious metal ... and beautiful stones hidden (would use these things).

"Supplying the vessels necessary for the solemn memorial of the sacrifice of the Son of God...

We know the kind of vessels in common use at the time, and recognize that the first 'paten' and chalice would very possibly be a tazza and a cup of silver or gold, perhaps adorned with gems and made beautiful in form and ornamentation. Tables of the same time often consisted of a marble slab supported by an ornamental frame of bronze ... Convenience would dictate that the table should be placed at the end of the room. The Apostles would naturally stand behind it as the ministrants, while the people would stand in reverent order in the body of the room, the men by themselves and the women by themselves; this was the arrangement dictated by our Lord. Look at the dress of the Apostles, for it is the earliest authority for clerical 'vestments.'

"The usual dress of the higher and middle classes at the time in Judaea, as elsewhere, was the tunic and pallium." (Footnote: "The pallium was an oblong piece of cloth, lately come into use instead of the old toga, and was disposed in certain folds about the person.")

"On occasions of religion and ceremony their colour was white, and the long tunic was worn, the sleeves of which reached to the wrists and the skirts to the ankles. This is the dress assigned to the Apostles in the earliest pictorial representations. Even when the successors of the Apostles had adopted other fashions of episcopal costume — and it is highly probable that it is that which they actually wore — it is a costume of such statuesque simplicity of line and breadth of fold that artists to this day employ it to give dignity to their sacred figures ... St. Peter is represented as saying: 'My dress is what you see, a tunic with a pallium.

(In large houses) "te caenaculum would contain at least one hundred and twenty persons ... An Eastern reception room has little more permanent furniture than the low bench which runs along one or more of its sides, so that there was nothing to interfere."

(With reference to the sanctuary vessels):

"In the costly beauty of the sacred vessels, in the habit of the ministers, in the order of the congregation, there was nothing lacking to the dignity of the divine service. We have taken pains to realize this assembly of the Apostle's Church ... the error that the early Church affected a studious plainness and informality in divine worship and its appointments ... the first Christians were Jews, and had been trained in the principles of the splendours of the Temple ... even the synagogues were handsome buildings and suitably furnished. The worship of the Church was the continuation of the solemn liturgical worship of the Temple. Probably the 'upper room' was the usual place of assembly of the innermost circle of Christ's disciples ... there the disciples assembled every day after the ascension...

"Christian congregations would pass through the outer court into the atrium — a lofty hall; two rows of pillars support the roof, which is open in the middle for light and air — the walls are divided by pilasters to correspond with the columns, and the wall panels are decorated with paintings ... At the farther end, when the curtain is withdrawn, the eye travels into the tablinum,"

(Footnote: "This custom of screening the tablinum from the atrium by a curtain was perhaps the origin of the custom of the early Church to place a curtain before the apse, which was drawn and withdrawn in different portions of the services") "which is like a chancel; its table is already conveniently placed for the approaching Breaking of the Bread; the necessary vessels are already placed upon it and the Apostle Paul and his assistant ministers, Silas and timotheus, are seated behind it, waiting to begin. The hall would be destitute of furniture, and the people would stand, the men with their heads uncovered, the women with the usual head veil, which partly concealed the face. There convenience would dictate that the divine service should be performed in the tablinum, and the sermon preached — thence people would come up to the tablinum and there, standing, would receive the consecrated food, as they do now in all the Churches of the East.

"No wonder that the place had become to them a sacred place 'none other than the house of God and the very Gate of Heaven.

"The Pudens saluted by St. Paul in his Epistle, 2 Tim. iv, 21, is said to have been the distinguished senator of that name, in whose house St. Paul is said to have lived, and the grandson of this Pudens, Pias I, Bishop of Rome A.D. 142 to 157, is said to have converted part of the family mansion," (Footnote: "Part of the house still remains" (Lanciani) "into a church of which the existing Church of St. Pudentiana is the successor. Its proper name is the Church of Pudens, and it is so called in an inscription on the book held by the figure of our Lord in the apse.

"There is reason to believe that the sumptuous appointments of the private houses ... sometimes possessed considerable wealth in gold and silver vessels for the Eucharistic service, silver lamps and silken hangings.

"Even in primitive times the Altar vessels, as chalices, patens, lamps, were of precious metals.

"Tertullian, in the latter part of the second century, speaks of the symbol of the good Shepherd on the Eucharistic cup, from which we infer that the chalices and probably other vessels were sometimes ornamented with symbols and pictures.

"... silver water-pots — a silver cumelinum (probably a flagon or bowl), and seven silver lamps."

WELLS AND GLASTONBURY ABBEY
BY THOMAS SCOTT HOLMES

Extract:

"It is the oldest ecclesiastical foundation in the island. It alone can claim that it forms the link between English and British Christianity. We must go deeper down; and how deep we cannot say, tracing back one tradition to ages long before the days of the Christian faith, where the heathen Celts and Brythons passed on from generation to generation their ideas and aspirations of another world and life. During the twelfth and thirteenth centuries ... two groups of legends spring up almost full-grown and attach themselves without difficulty to Glastonbury, the legend of St. Joseph of Arimathea, and the Holy Grail, and the legend of Arthur ... who was so popular in feudal times ...

"It was the Island of Glast or Aval, or Avallac, for such were the names of the gods who held sway in those regions of darkness and mystery. They thought also that in the distant island there was a mysterious cauldron of regeneraton into which the souls of heroes were dipped and whence they sprang into new life, healed of all their wounds ... as the solar myth, common to all the ancient religions of Indo-European races, linked itself on to these earlier legends, the setting and the rising sun, its death and its new birth helped to strengthen the faith of the Celt in the virtues of this new cauldron. But how were these legends connected with Glastonbury?.. In those remote ages the site was practically an island, and one of difficult approach except for small boats ... Now, if St. Joseph had the Grail, he must have taken it to Glastonbury, for all knew that at Glastonbury was the mystic vessel of regeneration — St. Joseph and the grail was the Christian form of the heathen legend.

"... The Welsh Triads belong to an age anterior to that in which they were put into writing, and they tell us there were three choirs of the Isle of Britain: the choir of Llan Iltud Vawr in Glamorganshire, the choir of Ambrosius in Ambresbury, and the choir of Glastonbury.

"In each of these three choirs ... there were 2,400 saints. So at Glastonbury there was a famous monastery several decades before the arrival of St. Augustine ... Nearly all the great saints of Celtic Christianity came and settled or were buried there.

"One fact ... he (Malmesbury) is able to adduce. The monks showed him an old document which was granted to the monastery by a king of Damnonia at the request of Abbot

Worgret, of the land of the island of Glastonbury, which came to be known as the Glastonbury twelve hides. This document was undated in 601, and we have in it convincing evidence that Glastonbury had been a Celtic monastery."

THE VICTIMS OF THE MARMERTINE
BY THE REV. A. J. O'REILLY, D.D.

Extract:

"THE APOSTLES IN THE MARMERTINE"

"Those who have seen the Marmertine, terrible in its modernized form, may conjure to the aid of imagination all that they may read of castle keeps, of dungeons, of dark cheerless cells, where the victims of injustice and tyranny have been cruelly immured.

"Yet the Marmertine could equal in the reality the gloomiest picture of fancy. Leave thy home and look into that cell that was never brightened by the cheerful ray of day, and behold the greatest heroes of the world chained to a column. Let not the darkness and fetid air drive you back, pass through the aperture in the rocky roof into the first prison, it is alone sufficient to terrify; but yet through another opening and descent into the lower dungeon — see the hard bed on which they sleep; behold the rock on which the Church of Jesus Christ has been built. The cold damp walls, the food of bread and water. Count the lonely hours and days passed for nine months in one dreadful night. No wonder St. Paul wrote: 'In chains for Jesus Christ.' The Apostle deprived Nero of his favourite concubine, and seduced his ablest secretaries. That is why they were kept so long confined in the Marmertine."

NERO EMPEROR OF ROME
BY ARTHUR WEIGALL

Extract from Page 259.

"Plots continued (i.e.: against Nero): presently it was reported to the Senate that a rebellion was being planned by Ostorius Scapula, a high military, who had distinguished himself in the wars in Britain but who of late had been under a cloud because he had allowed cartoons against Nero to be read at dinner parties. Another man involved was Publius Anteius. As soon as these men learnt that their plans had been discovered Anteius killed himself by taking poison, and Ostorius Scapula waited only for the arrival of the soldiers, and then ordering a slave to hold a sharp dagger to his throat, he flung himself upon it."

QUEEN ELIZABETH AND GLASTONBURY

"You hit us and our subjects in the teeth!" said Elizabeth to a Popish dignitary, "that the Romish Church first planted the Catholic faith within our realms; and records and chronicles of our realms testify the contrary; witness the ancient monument of Gildas, unto which both foreign and domestic have gone in pilgrimage there to offer.

"This author testifies Joseph of Arimathea to be the first preacher of God within our realms. Long after that, when Augustine came from Rome, these our realm, had bishops and priests therein, and is well known to the wise and learned of our realm by woeful experience, how your Church entered therein by blood, they being martyrs for Christ, and put to death, because they denied Rome's usurped authority."

BIBLIOGRAPHY

Lady Charlotte Guest; The Mabinogin.
Rev. G. Howard Wright, M.A.; Glastonbury and Rome — their true relationship, or is Rome our Mother?
Rev. S. Baring Gould, M.A.; The Lives of the Saints.
Butler; The Lives of the Saints (Illustrated — Universal History.
Hutchinson; The History of the Nations.
Rev. R.W. Morgan; St. Paul in Britain. The Origin of the British as opposed to Papal Christianity.
Rev. L. Smithett Lewis, M.A.; St. Joseph of Arimathaea at Glastonbury.
S. G. Davis *(The National Message);* Articles on the Druids.
F.W. Farrar; Darkness and Dawn.
Rudolfo Lanciani; Pagan and Christian Rome.
Rev. L. G. A.Roberts, Com. R.N.; British History traced from Egypt and Palestine, also the Anglo-Saxon original. Druidism in Britian. The Early British Church originally Hebrew.
Edward N. Cults; Early Christian Art.
Alice Cochran; The Dawn of British History.
Thomas Wright, Esq.; The Celt, the Roman and the Saxon.
J. W. Taylor; The Coming of the Saints.
Charles Squire; Mythology of the British Isles, Celtic Mythology and Legend, Poetry and Romance.
Rev. R. Douglas, M.A.; Darkest Britain's Epiphany.
Maj. J. Samuels, V.D., R.G.A.; The British Church (out of print).
Rev. A.J. O'Reilly, D.D.; The Victims of the Marmertine.
E. O. Gordon; Prehistoric London.
Charles Oman, K.B.E.; Castles, G.W.R. Holiday Haunts, G.W.R. South Wales — The Country and Castles, G.W.R.
Published by Arthur Young; Guide to Glastonbury.
Thomas Scott Holmes; Wells and Glastonbury Abbey.
Edward Blackhouse and Charles Taylor; Early Church History. "Fordington Monthly Messenger," March 1908, and Visitors' Souvenir of St.George's Prebendal Church, Fordington, Dorchester.
Rev. R. G. F. Waddington; Lecture on British Church.
H. J. Massingham; Pre-Roman Britain.
G. H. F. Nye; The Story of the Church of England. The Church and her Story. Usk, Monmouthshire (Guide).
Hutchinson; History of Cumberland.